Bristol Short Story Prize Anthology

Volume Eight

Bristol Short Story Prize Anthology Volume 8

First published 2015 by Tangent Books

Tangent Books
Unit 5.16 Paintworks
Bristol
BS4 3EH
0117 972 0645
www.tangentbooks.co.uk

Email: richard@tangentbooks.co.uk

ISBN: 9781910089231

Cover designed by Imogen Clifton
www.imogenclifton.com

Layout designed by Dave Oakley, Arnos Design
www.arnosdesign.co.uk

Printed and bound by ScandinavianBook.co.uk

A CIP catalogue record for this book is available from the British Library
www.tangentbooks.co.uk
www.bristolprize.co.uk

Contents

Introduction

The Bristol Short Story Prize is now eight years old, and attracts a wonderfully varied, imaginative and exciting range of writing from all over the English-speaking world. Nearly 2500 stories from 66 countries were submitted this year; judging them has been a real pleasure and a privilege.

Short stories are no longer the cinderellas of the fiction world. As well as an increasing number of outlets for publication and opportunities for prizes, short stories and collections occupy more shelf space in bookshops, more review space in newspapers, and more online territory than they have done for a long time. The internet has liberated stories from the page and opened up new ways of reaching readers. Short fiction suits modern life, and it's heartening to see just how many people want to write it and read it.

Enormous thanks are due to the team of first readers who sifted all the entries with a sharp eye and unflagging enthusiasm. Theirs was a real labour of love over many weeks, and they presented the judging panel with a longlist of forty very strong contenders. Whittling these down to twenty and choosing our three winners was difficult, but in the best possible way. We only decided on our shortlist after lengthy discussion; finding our winners involved even more discussion, much re-reading, and a good deal of individual advocacy by each of us.

It's not too difficult to pin down what makes a story good, but it's much harder to agree on what makes one good story better than another. We all felt our favourite stories included those moments when a paragraph, a sentence, or even just a few words, stood out as arresting and newly-made. Sometimes a story didn't make it to the final three but had moments that made us excited. For judge Sanjida O'Connell the stories *Flowers* and *Magpie* both have this quality of evocative, freshly-minted language: "I love their sparse descriptiveness, and the way both authors make skillful use of flora and fauna as metaphors for the action taking place."

We all liked the sensitive portrait of adolescent sexuality in *The Ice Ages*, the intensely personal treatment of a community's tragedy in *The Plait*, the unexpected take on the relationship between neighbours in *Just After We Stopped Talking*, the restrained and powerful exploration of an illegal immigrant's emotional trauma at the heart of *Black Lines*, the way that *Stafford Street* economically described the complex divisions of modern South Africa through the story of a woman's decision to move house.

Digital technology has made its mark on both subject matter and style, judge Nikesh Shukla points out: "The influx of social media, of digital connectedness in our lives made for a bunch of stories that narratively changed their structures to reflect modern ways of communication, miscommunication and representation." Rowan Lawton adds: "I was particularly struck by the darkness that runs through a number of the most impressive stories. In all three winning stories the authors handle this darkness with such a light touch that the stories feel even more impactful for it."

The story that wins third prize, *Birthday Bones*, has one of the best opening lines we read, and we knew we were in good storytelling hands from the start. It takes a very specific event and creates from it a story that has emotional depth and impact far beyond the circumstances of the event itself.

Between the Pickles, the second-prize winner, collides corporate America and immigration in the fast food industry with a confident gallows humour that we all relished. It is sharply and skillfully written, turning a surreal event into a politically astute and blackly funny story that is anchored in the everyday fear of an illegal immigrant's working life.

The first prize goes to *A Week on the Water*, a story that perfectly illustrates the art of narrative understatement. On the surface it's about fishing, but as it unfolds in measured, controlled prose, its real, horribly dark subject emerges. The narrative voice is deceptively cool, and the backstory is merely hinted at, from the first mention of being 'inside' to the final intimation of the reason the narrator is fishing on that particular stretch of city river.

All three prizewinning stories ended well, something that we came to look for increasingly as we worked through the longlist. There were a number of stories that kept us reading, only to let us down with weak or inconclusive endings. A good ending isn't necessarily a complete wrapping up of the story or a top-note finale, but a story needs an emotional resolution of some kind, so that as readers we feel we have reached an insight or understanding we didn't have when we began reading, that our investment in the story has paid off.

The Bristol Short Story Prize couldn't happen without the year-round hard work and enthusiasm of Joe Melia, who not only runs a smooth operation but does it with immense good cheer. His commitment to the short story form is formidable and inspiring, and he makes being part of the team a real pleasure. We are also grateful to Tangent Books for their professional involvement and support in publishing this anthology, and to Imogen Clifton, whose wonderful cover design was chosen from a selection submitted by talented final year students on the Illustration course at the University of the West of England. Thanks, also, to course leaders Chris Hill and Jonathan Ward at U.W.E. for making the cover design project such a fantastic experience.

And of course, more than anything, we are grateful to the many writers all round the world who sent in stories for this year's competition; you are keeping the lifeblood of the short story circulating. To the three prize-winners and the other writers included in this anthology, many congratulations. And to our readers, we hope you enjoy this selection of original, entertaining and thought-provoking stories from the 2015 Bristol Short Story Prize.

Sara Davies
September 2015

1ˢᵗ Prize
Brent van Staalduinen

Brent van Staalduinen lives, works, and finds his voice in Hamilton, Ontario, Canada. His novel *Chance & King* is forthcoming from Invisible Press in the spring of 2016. Other work is forthcoming in *The Prairie Journal* and *Prairie Fire Magazine* and appears in *EVENT Magazine, Litro Magazine, The Dalhousie Review, The New Quarterly, The New Guard Literary Review*, and *Mash Stories*. He is a graduate of the Humber School of Writers and holds an MFA in Creative Writing from the University of British Columbia.

A Week on the Water

A few weeks ago, I asked to work days but the manager just smirked. I told him it was a bitch to get buses up the escarpment late at night and that sleeping through the day made it hard to see my son. He balled up my kelly green apron and flung it against my chest. I almost dropped it, its ties cascading from my hands halfway to the floor like entrails. "Guess you shouldn't have messed up so bad, then," he said.

All you can do is ask, I think, waiting for the tip of my fishing rod to dance.

I don't argue any more. It's a hard habit to break but that former edge, the strongest and most successful part of myself, won't help me. Better for it to sit in my stomach like a river stone - one of the native guys inside said that if you swallow enough of them the appetite goes away. He didn't seem like he was particularly plugged in to the spirit side of things and was probably making things up as he went – like all of us – but I guess the idea works just fine, apart from wondering where the stones will end up.

"Greenie still giving you grief?"

Gram's cigarette dances on his lower lip with every syllable. I met him almost a week ago. He's out fishing every day too.

"Always," I say.

"That whole place is green," he said on Tuesday. I had just told him about the supermarket where I worked nights and he went straight to the colour scheme. I didn't say much, but I told him about the manager who makes me sign my paycheque over to him every two weeks then pays me in cash, significantly reduced. "After taxes," he always says with a sneer. Yesterday, Gram decided to call him Greenie.

He spits.

"God, I hate that part of the city. Did I tell you I used to have a house up there, right across the street from all those big box stores?"

"No," I say.

He smiles. His teeth used to be perfect, I can see.

"Yeah, paid for that bad boy in cash. All those fat, bored housewives looking for a little something. Suburban junkies – best market ever."

"You don't live up there any more."

A dark look deepens his features, fleeting, and he gives a lipless smile. But he doesn't reply. You learn not to ask when they're not offering, so I take a small piece of chicken liver and thread it onto the treble hook.

We're on the harbour side of the fishway, next to the recreation path, dropping for catfish. The secret is the bait; it has to be smelly and full of proteins so the cats can find it. Gram's working some old Fancy Feast cat food in surgical tubing and he's had better luck. He said I could try some of his, but my grandfather swore by liver and I'm stubborn about these things. Still, I haven't caught a thing, a week of lob cast after lob cast and waiting while the current dilutes the juices in the meat before having to do it all over again. There's something about loyalty, though.

I don't mind the job, despite my douchebag boss. The store's open twenty-four hours a day but most of the restocking happens overnight, when there are fewer customers to get in the way. They have to pay a night manager, a cashier, and a small army of guys who need to work at night: even though they only open one checkout and dim the lights in the storeroom I can't imagine how they make any money. Not my call – in my former life I'd have cringed at the business model, unknowing that one moment of weakness and seven long years would erase the need to worry about anything greater than working a night shift, getting to bed afterwards, and channel fishing as daily therapy.

Gram's rig dips and drifts. He picks it up from the little rack he's spiked into the ground and holds it away from himself, eyes closed, feeling the bite. A quick upward pull to set the hook and the fish, feeling the tug, tries to run towards the harbour. It's all over in less than a minute. Such a narrow channel and there's nowhere to go, and the fish can't fathom the disparity in physics between the rod and reel and its own finite strength. It's a good one, three or four pounds, and Gram lifts it out of the water with a thumb in its gaping mouth. A thin line of bright red blood runs down its grey belly and drips steadily onto the gravel shoreline. The fish gives a weak twitch of its tail, flinging blood all over.

"Ah, shit, I hate it when they bleed," he says, holding the cat away from his body and wiping the hem of his rain jacket.

"He'll bleed out, I think."

"Yeah, we hooked the gills."

Using the treble hook is a conscious choice. Cats almost always swallow the small trebles whole and the points work hell on their insides. Some guys bend and break off the barbs at each razor point but we don't, preferring a good hook set to the more sporting approach of catch-and-release. Gram likes the taste of catfish but admits that he's too lazy to take them home and clean them. I'd do it, but the halfway house frowns on the mess and smell of gutting and frying the catch. If they live, we toss them back into the channel; if they don't, we leave them out for the birds and animals to take care of. But it's been a cold few days, so maybe the animals can't smell the ones Gram gill hooked and left to die pale, bloodless deaths.

We still have the conversation we've had all week, though.

"You gonna do something with this one?"

"Can't," he says.

"Me neither."

On Wednesday, I learned that Gram changed his name after he dropped out from college to deal full-time ("I used to be a Graham," he laughed. "Get it?"). It was a really slow fishing day, kind of windy and choppy on the harbour side, so we set up on the marsh side next to the fishway. They set up a barrier across the Desjardins Canal to act like a sieve, keeping the mature carp, big suckers who feed on the bottom, from swimming in and upsetting the plant life. Hard to believe one species can ruin so much water. I don't think either of us got even a nibble from the native marsh fish. Gram did most of the talking that day. Most days, actually – not arguing so much any more leaves a lot less for me to say.

Gram pulls out a joint the size of my pinkie and asks if I want to spark up. I shake my head, conscious of the weekend cyclists and rollerbladers hissing past.

"Relax, man, we're too far down the trail."

He giggles – a grating sound in the cool air – and tries to light it. It's calm today, the birds making perfect mirror images of themselves on the channel, but damp too, so the J won't stay lit. After a few tries he swears, the scorched tip bouncing like the head of an impatient, greasy maggot.

Then it's the tip of my rod bowing towards the algae-green water and I'm up trying to set the hook. But it pulls too easy. I missed the hit, figure the cat must've nabbed the liver and spat it out before I could hook him. I reel it in, the bright sinker emerging from the underwater gloom followed by the leader and treble. Bare, as though the fish's tongue was able to weave itself around and through the barbs gently enough to take the bait but not get caught.

"Took my bait," I say as I pinch and skewer another bit of bloody liver.

Gram doesn't say anything. Unusual. Just before I lob out my rig, I look over at him. He's zoned right out, staring at the far bank, through the ground, maybe, or into the past he talks about so much I wonder if he's lying. Just to have a story. I knew guys like that inside, so wrecked they'd talk and talk even after getting beaten up for saying the wrong thing. There was this one guy who walked up to the new ones at intake and told each of them a different story about how he ended up there. One day I watched him get his head caved in by a skinhead who probably wasn't even listening but needed to hurt someone anyhow.

I wave my hand in front of his face. Nothing.

"Don't bother when he gets like that – too much of his own product for too long," a voice says from behind.

A pair of bike cops, top-heavy in body armour and utility belts and bright yellow jackets, have ridden up without a sound and stopped at the edge of the paved path behind us. Spindly legs, ridiculous black socks and safety shoes, wraparound sunglasses. I almost laugh but the J is still hanging from Gram's mouth, and the one who spoke, the bigger one, looks like the type to get worked up over a single joint.

"Isn't that right, Gram?"

Gram blinks a few times and turns towards the cops. He gives a dopey smile, looks past the big one, and tilts his head in a hopeful greeting towards the other guy.

"Hey, Wharton."

"Gram."

Wharton, the smaller one who's as pale as our dead fish on the shoreline, says this without taking his eyes from the water on the other side of the fishway. He leans across the handlebars of his police-issue mountain bike and simply studies Cootes Paradise like he's thinking about taking his next

15

holiday there. Gram slips the J into his pocket, but neither of the cops says anything about that. He fidgets. A tight soundtrack of spare change and hidden keys. The big guy nods at me and asks me my name.

The new me grits his teeth and tells him.

"Holy fuck! Almost a week of fishing and I never even knew his name!"

Gram's too excited, hoping this new interesting tidbit will distract everyone, maybe. The big cop dismounts, clicks down the kickstand and steps unevenly across the stones to the edge of the water. Turns towards me, takes off his glasses, and scratches a patch of missed stubble with a fingernail. The arms of his Oakleys swing and knock against his chin with each scratch.

"Anything biting?"

"Not today, no."

Now that he's closer he looks even bigger. His expensive sunglasses have stencilled tan lines on his cheekbones. I don't have to ask to know there are equally sharp lines on his thick biceps and thighs and calves; a creature of routine, every item of uniform put on the same way every time. He doesn't look like the type of guy to be a bike cop – he'd look more at home squeezed behind the steering wheel of one of those smaller new cruisers and harassing kids on skateboards.

"We heard you were out," he says. "Shame they couldn't put you somewhere else."

Wharton is ignoring the waves of cliché his partner is putting out. He's closed his eyes and turned his face towards the muddy sun trying to peek through the clouds. Gram fidgets next to me, a sparrow trying not to get noticed as it hops between tables looking for crumbs. I don't say anything, just dangle the liver-baited rig over the water and lob it out. It sinks without a ripple. I sit back down onto my blue Igloo cooler.

"Are we going to have any trouble with you?"

I shake my head, taking exactly one second for each side to keep the redness from blinding me.

"No, sir."

"No, sir," Gram parrots.

As the big one nods and starts back to his bike, Wharton begins to speak, never opening his eyes or turning his face away from the warmth he's found, and suddenly I know which of these two I'm really going to have to worry about.

"See, that's the thing about the big ones – trafficking, rape, homicide – what actually happens looks so different after the courts get done with it."

Two of those were meant for me. Gram took the other in with a little whimper, his brag and bluster dissolved like sugar in hot water.

"And it concerns me to find you here, close enough to the home you've been ordered to stay away from that it's obvious you're not ready to move on, but far enough away that you could honestly say it's about the fishing."

Gram's shoulders relax and he studies the place where his line disappears into the water. I can almost hear him clueing in that the cops aren't really concerned about him at all.

"Your record says you're smart. Clever too, maybe. But, then, I was never a fan of clever," Wharton finishes.

I don't argue any more, I want to say.

Wharton opens his eyes and takes another long look at the calm water on the other side of the fishway, waiting for his partner to mount his bike. Then the cops pedal slowly away, nodding and smiling at the pedestrians and other cyclists on the harbour side of the path, ringing their handlebar bells for the kids. Gram fishes quietly beside me having decided, I know, to wait until later to Google his new fishing friend. I probably won't see him tomorrow, Sunday, my last day of work and fishing before my Monday off. I'll go back to hooking channel cats on my own and watching the path, hoping someone in that home will decide that it's a nice enough day for a walk, maybe, down by the marsh.

2nd Prize
J.R. McConvey

J.R. McConvey is a writer based in Toronto, Canada. He is the author of an e-book, *The Last Ham*, published by House of Anansi Digital. His short fiction has appeared in *The Malahat Review, Joyland, EVENT, The Dalhousie Review, The Puritan* and other outlets, and his stories have been shortlisted for the Matrix Lit POP award and the Thomas Morton Memorial Prize. He also publishes assorted bits of poetry and journalism, and regularly reviews books for *The Globe and Mail*. He is on Twitter @jrmcconvey and online at jrmcconvey.wordpress.com.

Between The Pickles

1.

You're just the Wrapper, Rosa. That's what they told you. Your one job, your only job, is to wrap the sandwiches in waxed paper and slide them down the metal chute and that's it. Any problems and you're gone.

The thing stares out at her from between the two flaccid pickle slices like a hairless mouse. She caught it just as she was folding the first logoed flap over the spongy white bun, stopped short and gasped and summoned every bit of strength she had to stifle a shriek. Now she's just standing there, sweat soaking the back of her polyester uniform, every second that ticks by bringing her closer to the questions from her manager that she can't afford to answer. *What the hell is that? How did it get there?*

She wants, as bad as anything she's ever wanted, for the thing to be innocent, a rotten carrot or a stray piece of cattle bone that got missed in the grinding. But there's no mistaking it: the nail, the knuckle, the wavy lines of fingerprint, swollen and grey but still readable as the map of an individual body, maybe dead but maybe alive somewhere and wondering what became of its missing digit. Never dreaming that it would end up here, at Pancho's Escondido, nestled into the middle of an Azteca Burger with cheese, threatening to fuck up everything Rosa García has been working for over the past nine months.

Dios mio. Rosa feels hot acid rising up her gorge. She clenches her fists, presses fingernails into palms. Repeats the refrain in her head – the one they gave her, but also the longer one, the one she's made for herself, which she recites to keep her going whenever things look like they might start turning to shit again.

You're just the Wrapper. You're just the Wrapper. You're just the Wrapper, this is your only job. It's not even the job that matters: it's the paycheque. Focus on the paycheque, Rosa, hold it in your mind like the face of Jesus Christ, because it's the thing that's going to save you – from *La Migra's* guns, searchlights whiter and hotter than the Chihuahuan noon, fear rusting your stomach like a heavy chain while you try not to breathe, try to stop existing for as long as it takes for them to move on to the scent of some other poor bastard cowering out there in the desert, half dead from terror and thirst. From the house back in Jalapa, Mama's bloody coughs rattling like wet bones in the kitchen, the smells of fever and rot and dust coming off her skin. From the sting of Angel's hand on your cheek when you cried for your dying mother, and from how you went limp when he threw you onto the sofa.

She thinks about Diego, back at the apartment, sleeping in his crib while Valentina watches the evening news beside him, as peaceful and radiant a scene as any holy book could promise.

The finger points at her, demanding a response. Even if it has nothing to do with her, even if it's just bad luck, it doesn't matter. *Illegal equals expendable.* Her manager's exact words. She'd had to look up the last one.

They'd have her on a southbound truck within an hour.

The hiss of a frozen patty hitting the griddle brings her back to present time. Like that, she decides. Don't move, don't breathe. Head down. Just like in the desert, let it pass you by.

Rosa swallows hard to quell the puke feeling and puts on her best company face – no problems here, señor – lifts the waxed paper over the nightmare to cover its horror with the friendly PANCHO'S logo, folds the greasy flaps under to seal the deal, and slides the sandwich down the metal chute and, she hopes, out of her life forever. She dings the bell, order ready, and tries to fade back into the haze of frying oil and grill smoke filling the kitchen like a tropical mist.

Remember, Rosa. You're just the Wrapper.

2.

He's weighing how far to go.

It took more than enough effort to suppress the initial gag reflex when he bit into it and felt the bone. To not panic once he drew it back and saw the thing buried in there, poking out just enough that it looked for all the world like his Azteca Burger was sticking out its tongue at him. To lift off the top bun and peel up the sour greyish flap that passed for a pickle and confirm what his incisors already knew: that there was a *human finger* in his lunch food, slathered in ketchup and Sombrero Sauce and a smattering of diced onions.

But what was absolutely heroic, absolutely fucking Herculean, was that Mike Stevens was still just sitting there looking at it, trying to decide on the best way forward. That he had the wherewithal to fight back disgust and take a rational look at the situation. To take a deep breath and imagine the kind of shit-show that would erupt, the kind of irreparable damage that would occur, if he were to stand up in the middle of the restaurant and scream like a baby and have to explain, first to the TV cameras and then to Head Office, that the beloved Pancho's chain was so lax in its food handling practices that this grotesque tidbit had managed to travel from whatever cursed slaughterhouse it had come from, all the way down the delivery chain, to end up on his tray, in his burger, in his mouth.

Mike closes his eyes for a minute, running his fingers down the length of his tie, trailing grease. Everyone knows fourth quarter revenues are dragging the bottom. Everyone's heard about what happened over at KBC-Flaxos after JerryBurger went tits up. If the axe falls at SitcoBVM, junior execs will be the first on the chopping block.

All that work, all that eating shit, all that proverbial licking of Carl Drais' ballsack, for nothing. The resort vacation next month? Forget it. Never mind the family he and Kara have been talking about having, maybe a year down the road. All of a sudden he's not *father material*, just another dud in a bargain suit pleading his way through dozens of job interviews and eating Ritz crackers and spreadable cheese for lunch.

Forget it. That's the thing to do. Forget it. Stand up, walk over to the trash and dump the thing into the bin, erase it from memory. Take one for the team.

He opens his eyes and looks over to the counter and notices the Mexican girl staring at him. She's crouched at the wrapping station, where the burgers get packaged and slid out onto the metal chute to be organized into orders, peering over a row of yellow-wrapped Bandito Burritos with eyes as wide and black as tar pits.

She knows.

She saw it, and she served it anyway. Is fully, 100% aware what kind of horror-show she's just pushed through the line to be turned into someone's lunch, someone else's problem. Jesus. What the fuck was she thinking?

Mike answers the question before it's even finished forming in his mind. She's pretty. Pretty Mexican girl. Skin the colour of toasted almond, big pouty lips, wide, nervous eyes that have probably seen down the business end of a border guard's assault rifle on occasion. Illegal, no doubt. She pukes or screams or breaks down weeping, causes any kind of a scene, the questions start flying, and she's back across the border faster than you can say *ándale arriba*.

He fidgets with his tie again, has to stop himself from putting it between his teeth to chew on while he sorts it all out. The tie was a gift from Kara, Egyptian silk.

What if this Mexican chick can't hold it together? What if she wakes up thrashing from a nightmare of bloody digits crawling across her skin like maggots, and spills? Who gets asked questions then?

So, Mike thinks, staring back at her, trying to sound confident in his head – deep-voiced, like Drais. *We find ourselves at a crossroads.* The question is, what's he willing to gamble? What happens if he chucks the thing, wipes it from memory, and she does the same – and he still ends up as a redundancy, a little red mark in the SitcoBVM ledger, just a severance package away from starting over again? Kara's been crystal clear on this point: lose the job, lose her. Lose everything. Become a loser. He is not naïve about the allure of his platinum cards.

Fuck it, he thinks in the Drais voice. *You want to get to the top of the food chain, you'd better learn how to chew.*

Mike Stevens, Junior VP of Marketing for the Pancho's Restaurant Division of SitcoBVM, gives the Mexican girl one last glance, then lifts his eyes up to the backlit menu on the wall behind the counter and recites in his head, as benediction and penance, the hallowed names of PANCHO'S trademarked product line: Azteca Burger™, Bandito Burrito™, Torero Chicken™, Taco Fantastico™, Bordertown Chili Fries™, amen. He picks up the sandwich and sinks his teeth down through the whole girth of it as hard as he can, taking a huge bite, snapping through bone, pumping his jaw up and down until the fragment of finger he's torn off has been ground into oblivion, and, making sure she's still watching, swallows with only a barely perceptible flinch. The rest he wraps up and shoves into his satchel, the fate of his career congealing in its blasphemed, mustardy innards. He takes a huge swig of cola and leaves his tray on the table when he gets up to go, a scattering of too-crisp fries cast like divining bones across the translucent paper of the promotional mat.

3.

"You're fucking kidding me, right? Fucking *kidding* me."

Carl Drais stares at the soggy pile of dogshit besmirching his oak desk and tries to process the story this lesser minion sitting across from him has just disgorged.

"No sir," says the minion, Mike something-or-other. "No joke, I'm afraid."

"Afraid is the right word, son. Do you have any idea what you're telling me?"

"Yes, sir."

"Do you understand, not just the health code violations that have been perpetrated here, the potential billions in lawsuits, but also how personally fucking disgusted I am at what you've done?"

"I only had the company's best interests in mind, sir."

Carl Drais puts his hands together and leans back in his chair, a move he's practiced hundreds of times.

"And I presume you can explain exactly how this particular bit of personal deviance will benefit a multinational conglomerate like SitcoBVM?"

"Well, sir," says minion Mike, "I think it's all a matter of perspective. It was easy to see what a disaster this could turn into for the company" –

"What a keen observation!"

"But with a little creativity, it occurred to me that we might be looking at an opportunity here."

Carl frowns, folding his thick brows into an arachnoid ridge. "What I'm looking at is a half-masticated cheeseburger with a fucking zombie finger wedged between the pickles, and a lunatic cannibal shitbag telling me he's *eaten* half the finger in the name of shareholder gains!"

Carl counts out the seconds of silence, watching minion Mike tremble in his chair, smelling the sour sweat leaking from his armpits. He needs the fear. If he doesn't break this man thoroughly – if he lets on too early that he is, in fact, intrigued – things could easily go haywire, as in bankruptcy for the corporation, as in jail time, contraband cigarettes, dropped soap and death by Pruno. No idea is anathema to Carl if he can see the money… and there's something here, for sure. Why not? When you know what the fucking beef farms look like, this isn't a stretch at all. It just might be the game changer, the thing they remember him for. Put his name up there with Ray Kroc and Dave Thomas and the goddamn A&W bear. He has to retain total control, though, complete mastery of the situation, or he runs a major risk of turning into a scapegoat for a board of directors that would pulp their own mothers to save their hides, if anyone were to find out that Pancho's has been accidentally serving up anonymous human appendages in its Buenos Combos. To work, this has to look intentional.

Eight… nine… ten… Tick-tick. Spidery seconds. He lets them crawl all over minion Mike, get into his ears. Get him primed to do anything Carl wants.

"Now," says Carl. "The first thing is, why should I even believe you? How do I know you're not here to set me up somehow? You come in here making a claim like this, you'd better be ready to back it up without question."

"But the burger, sir—"

"Came out of your cheap man purse, and could be made of fucking plasticine, for all I know. If I'm inferring correctly, here, it's going to take a more immediate display of your commitment to the campaign to get me to agree to even poke it with a sterilized ten-foot pole. Brand loyalty starts with the executive, son. You want to sell this thing? You want to convince me it's not just the whim of some deranged pervert? You want to push this kind of radical product on Pancho's ever-fickle customer base? You have to prove to me you can love it, first and foremost."

Carl watches minion Mike's face turn pale as bleached flour.

"So," Carl says, leaning in, glancing down at the tepid mass of dry beef, modified corn syrup, wilted vegetables and human biology nestled in a manger of cheese-caked Pancho's parchment. "Have another bite."

Carl Drais watches his soon-to-be-slightly-less-minor-minion absorb the request, digest the inevitable and steel himself for round two. Truth is, there's so much salt on those goddamn burgers that you could throw a nuclear cow turd on top and most people would never taste the difference. The real challenge will be marketing, and of course convincing the FDA yahoos, but such is the fast food business. That's what Carl Drais has been doing his whole life.

In less than a year, he'll be out, southward bound, blowing his fat retirement package on pig roasts, mojitos and fishing gear for his Caribbean yacht, *Delilah*. But what good will it be, if no one remembers him? Carl has always wanted to shake things up. To really *change* things. Truth is, he'd give up every last penny in his accounts if he knew it would mean the name Carl Drais making its way into textbooks across the country.

When minion Mike chomps down on the sandwich, looking only slightly paler at actually eating the thing than he did at the suggestion of eating it, Carl knows he's got something he can work with. He watches, silent as a big cat, as Mike chews, his face cycling through the stages of guilt, shame, denial and acceptance with each roll of the fleshy slurry around his tongue. And when Mike finally swallows, an almost convincing look of greasy satisfaction on his face, Carl smiles.

"Well," he says. "I must say, you look like you quite enjoyed that."

"Yes, sir."

"Listen, Mike – what was your last name again?"

"Stevens, sir."

"Listen, Mike. I must say, on witnessing your unbridled commitment to this new product, I'm warming to it. I'm thinking we may have something here."

Mike Stevens' eyes light up, all the lingering disgust melted away in a ping of hope and newly stoked ambition, and Carl Drais knows that he's got him. Now it's just the final touch, the conspiratorial about-face, and he'll have Stevens ready to eat an entire bucket's worth of deep-fried baby fingers at the flick of his lapel.

"Of course, I'm going to want some time to digest it all. So I'll ask that you leave me now, to see where I can get with it. But, on the way out, you'll want to tell Sheena to order you up some new business cards. If you're going to be handling an account this, let's say, touchy, we'll need you to have access to resources beyond what junior VP clearance allows for." Carl smiles, spider brows relaxed into a pair of friendly salt-and-pepper caterpillars.

"Yes, sir. Thank you, sir."

"And Mike?"

"Yes sir."

"I'll need you for another meeting tomorrow. After that, you take yourself a bit of a vacation. Maui, or Antigua. Somewhere nice."

"Yes, sir."

When Stevens is gone, Carl Drais picks up the half-eaten sandwich from his desk, a tidbit of finger the length of a thimble still plugged in among the oozing condiments. He wafts the burger under his nose, taking in its musk, gauging its appeal – coaxing, from amidst the scents of grease and onion and vinegar, the rarefied aura, the decadent essence that can reveal to him the secret of how to introduce this, his newest baby, to a hungry world.

4.

They told her not to worry, but holy shit is she worried. Worry is a primary ingredient in Rosa's life, but this is worse than the usual kind, the one she gets when old white men look at her too hard or whenever she passes a policeman on the street. This is sick worry, you-know-what-you-did worry. You-got-yourself-into-some-kind-of-serious-shit worry. You've-been-caught worry. Why else would she be here in the waiting room of SitcoBVM headquarters, told flat out that her presence was not optional? Why else would she be waiting for a meeting with the CEO, a guy she'd never heard of before the company reps showed up at her door telling her that he was 'a man of national importance?' Why else would they even have bothered to track down her address, which she had never given the company because her manager paid her under the table in cash? *It's not even a paycheque, Rosa. It's an envelope he hands to you at the end of the week on your way out the door. Paycheques are for real people. Legal people.* Why else would Carl Drais want to talk to a woman who didn't even exist?

Diego coos and dribbles on her shoulder. She wonders why she bothered putting on the red dress, the only good one she owns, when she knows it's just going to get covered in spit-up. It's bad enough that Valentina's working and she has to carry Diego with her into the lion's den; she had to go and put on lipstick, too. Who gets dressed up to be arrested? But that leads her back to the question that confuses her most, the one that always wedges itself between her and the heavy prison door she keeps imagining swinging in to bang shut over the rest of her life: why didn't they just send the police to her house? Why bring someone like her into their fancy glass-walled offices?

The receptionist's phone buzzes and she picks it up and nods twice, looking in Rosa's direction, saying "Hmm, yessir." She hangs up and smiles at Rosa.

"Mr. Drais will see you now."

Rosa puts a hand on the back of Diego's little head and stands up. What can she do? Run? Running is what got her here. On shaky legs, she carries her son past the big wooden reception desk that reminds her of a coffin, and walks through the huge doors into the office of Carl Drais, CEO.

"Good afternoon," says the man standing behind the desk, a tall man whose hair is like polished grey bone. She looks over into the corner and sees another guy, and when she recognizes him as the one from Pancho's, the one who ate the bad sandwich, she has to blink hard and steady herself to keep from fainting and dropping Diego onto the hardwood.

"Rosa, correct? Rosa Garcia. We've been learning a lot about you."

His smile is like a cheese-grater buffed to a perfect shine. The other man sits quietly in the corner, dead still.

"Please don't be alarmed," says Carl Drais in a honey-smoked tone. "Mr. Stevens and I realize what you're probably thinking, but I assure you, we have no intention of reprimanding you, or exploiting your, let us say, documentational circumstances. In fact" – he pauses and comes around the desk, and Rosa reflexively hugs Diego to her chest – "what we'd like do to is offer you an opportunity."

Now his hand is on her shoulder. If he touches Diego, she'll rip at his throat, scratch and bite him bloody, tear him piece by piece until the other one brains her from behind with a paperweight, or just reaches in and touches the barrel of his silenced pistol to her temple to bury a bullet in her skull, like they do in the Mafia movies. But Carl Drais' hand stays resting on her upper arm, giving the gentlest squeeze.

"We think you may have, however inadvertently, pointed toward a bold new direction for the Pancho's restaurant chain."

He runs his fingers down her arm to her hand, and he lifts it, his palm cool and dry against her hot, damp one, until its sits, flat and brown and trembling between them. She's shaking, holding Diego close enough to her that he fuses to her skin, so that there's no way they can tear him from her, with all of it running through her head again: the desert and the dogs and the paycheque and the finger and the night retching in guilt and terror afterward, the men coming to her door, the red dress, the waiting room, and now here, with Carl Drais, which could be worst of all.

"With the right product testing and market research, and of course the small challenge of navigating a few outdated regulations with our friends at the FDA, we believe we might be looking at the next flagship Pancho's sandwich. Still in the earliest stages of development, of course – but for the moment, we're thinking of calling it 'The Dream'."

The one who ate it, Mr. Stevens, stands and walks over to them and looks her in the eyes while he fiddles with his tie. He's younger, and there's something in his own eyes that's not quite fear, not quite nervousness, but a kind of retreat, as though he's pulling back into himself, back into the flesh and muscle of his big, solid Midwestern body.

"But of course all of this is only possible with your full cooperation," says Carl Drais. "We can make sure you're well taken care of – take away any question of your right to belong in this nation of ours, give you a permanent position in company – but you also must understand that the privilege of liberty, so to speak, does not come without a certain sacrifice."

Carl Drais lifts her hand up right close to his face and for a second she thinks he might kiss, it, but he just wafts it under his nose, inhaling deeply.

"So what do you think, Rosa?" he says. "How would you like to be more than just a Wrapper?"

Mr. Stevens clears his throat. Diego coughs spittle. Rosa swallows, opens her mouth, blinks. She's remembering the first time she ever ate a Pancho's burger, the day Valentina moved in and they treated themselves to a couple of Pequeño Combos. The way they'd touched their burgers together in a makeshift toast, wrinkled their noses as they chewed the first bites, feeling the salt tingling on their tongues, the limp pickles squeaking between their teeth. How they'd laughed, almost rejoicing in the luxury of throwing away half their lunches. Shaking their heads, saying, what a country. What a country, this.

3rd Prize
Magdalena McGuire

Magdalena McGuire was born in Poland, grew up in Darwin, and now lives in Melbourne with her husband and her collection of vintage dresses. She is an avid reader and particularly enjoys reading books about girls who like reading books. Magdalena has published widely on human rights topics, including women's rights and the rights of people with disabilities. Her fiction has been published by *The Big Issue* and Margaret River Press. You can say hello to her on Twitter at @Magdalena_McG.

Birthday Bones

It was the day before castration day and the island was teeming. People were loading cages into trucks to take to the local school. Dogs paced the streets as though anxious about what tomorrow would bring.

Ange was paying her yearly visit to the island butcher: a heavyset man rumoured to have a hoard of illegitimate children living on the mainland. He rung up the till for another customer while Ange waited in front of the display of a pig's head nested on fake grass, its naked grin pointing her way. Tomorrow, as well as being castration day, was her dog's birthday. Every year on her birthday, Ruby was allowed a couple of cow bones – a diversion from her regular diet of brown rice and kale.

'So, two legs for the birthday girl,' the butcher said with a wink. He scanned Ange's shorts and she moved her shopping bag in front.

'Actually, this year I need a whole bag of bones. I'm helping out with tomorrow–'

'Ah, castration day. You're joining in the fun!' The butcher grabbed his crotch, leaving behind a fresh streak of blood.

'Yeah,' said Ange, her eyes fixed on the streak. 'That's one way of looking at it.'

When Ange first arrived on the island, ten years ago, there were just enough dogs to lend the place an air of charm, like the cats of Cypress.

Back then, the island dogs lived well enough, feeding on leftover curry and rice and the expensive tinned food the tourists sometimes bought. But now there were too many dogs. Everywhere you went: desperate, deranged-with-hunger dogs who snarled through yellow teeth, their ribs pushing through ravaged skin. Tourist children (their little pink bodies clad in tie-dye and batik) grew afraid. Complaints were made to hotel managers. 'Someone needs to do something about those dogs,' the tourists would say. 'We came here for a nice *family holiday*.'

There were no cars on the island. People used small trucks for carting around building materials or tourists, and scooters for their own use. Ange's scooter, once red, was faded pink by the sun and bitten with rust by the ocean air. Now she sat on the scooter, wedged the bag of frozen bones between her calves, and took off. Wind rushed about her face, whipping her hair as she took the curve of the gravel path up and down the hills.

To her right was the jungle. Trees and vines forced their way from a cliff face that had been sliced in half to accommodate the road. She passed a group of workers, bare chested, their t-shirts tied to their heads, shielding the sun. The men were using sickles to hack back the plants from the road. The plants on the island were growing, growing all the time – it was ferocious, their hold on life. If the humans ever had to evacuate, the plants would take over in weeks, consuming the roads and the houses in a tangled emerald mass. And everything man-made would be buried.

Leaning into a corner, Ange pulled a stray hair from her mouth and craned her neck to see the ocean. It lay behind the squat banana trees, a flat line of blue. Mountains jutted out of the horizon like peaks in a heart monitor. The inner pulse of the island, brought into view.

'Maphit!' Ange called to her husband as she walked along the veranda.

Squatting on the concrete, paint splattered on his chest and the tips of his dreadlocks, Maphit was working on a portrait of one of the island women – the wife of a white hotel owner. The woman bathed by a waterfall, bubbles floating around her, while a lizard stalked the edge of the river, a flick of tongue sticking out of its lip.

'Look out.' Maphit pointed a paintbrush her way. 'Here comes the bone lady.'

Ange leaned down to kiss him while Ruby scrabbled about, trying to get at the bones. 'My God, smell it.' Ange jiggled the bag in front of Maphit's face. 'It took two seconds for this to defrost in the heat.'

'Mmm,' Maphit said, and gave her a facetious grin. 'Those dogs may be losing their balls, but at least they get a good meal out of it.'

'Hey, it's not just the boys – the girls are getting de-sexed too.'

'It's worse for men. Anyway, not *all* the girls are getting it done.' He rolled back and forth on the balls of his feet, waiting for her response.

Ange turned and put the bag of bones on the table. 'We've been over this,' she said. In fact, they'd been over it and over it. It was cruel, allowing street dogs to breed. What was the point of bringing more of them into a world where they would starve and be kicked around by local business owners? But a dog who belonged to someone – that was different. That was family.

Ruby made a whinnying sound before sitting with a thump and holding up her front leg. She only had the one: the other front leg had been amputated after she'd been hit by a truck in the middle of the night. Whenever Ruby was in need of something – food, a walk – she would hold up her solitary front paw, reminding Ange of her affliction.

'Your birthday's not til tomorrow,' Ange said, hands on her hips. But the look on Ruby's face was pure hope. 'Oh alright.' Ange took a bone from the bag. 'There you go baby girl.'

Ruby clenched her jaws on the bone and ran to the garden with her lopsided gait. She lay down near her favourite spot – the large flat rock at the back. On the rock was a jar that Ange kept filled with flowers: hibiscus, bougainvillea, frangipani. Ruby chewed the bone, her eyes closed in concentration.

'You spoil that dog,' Maphit said. He turned back to his canvas and added a touch of brown to the woman's nipple.

That night, Ange lay in bed thinking about tomorrow. Twelve vets had been ferried over from the mainland to help out with the operations. Ange and the other volunteers had one day to collect as many dogs as they could and transport them to the makeshift clinic at the school. There, the dogs would be de-sexed and fitted with plastic tags to show they could no longer breed. Rumour had it that, after castration day, any dog without a plastic tag in their ear would be shot on sight. 'Of course, domestic pets need to be neutered as well,' the island vet had pointed out. 'Of course,' Ange said.

It was late when Ange fell asleep, only to be woken by a roar in the sky. Rain hurtled down on the thatched roof and against the bamboo walls, finding its way in through the gaps.

The sun was already fierce at nine in the morning, the coolness of last night's rain having been swallowed by the humidity. Ange, her eyes bulging with lack of sleep, was wearing her hangover glasses: wide, fake Pradas she'd bought from one of the vendors on the beach. At least her friend Tara would be driving.

Although Tara had lived on the island for longer than Ange, she had never succumbed to the local uniform of singlet and shorts. Today, Tara wore flowing pink trousers and a white shirt, buttoned to her neck. Driving, she had one hand on the wheel and waved the other as she complained about her husband. 'So of course he's too busy to help out today. Maphit too, I take it? They complain about these dogs, then leave the dirty work to us.'

'Actually,' Ange said, 'Maphit had to go to the mainland to sell some paintings.'

'And it just had to be done today?' Tara arched an eyebrow.

'Well…'

'There you go. It's the same when it comes to the kids. I'm the one who has to stop them running wild. They need *boundaries*, right? Especially in a place like this.'

'Well that's right,' Ange said. 'I always said to Maphit that our ki–' She stopped, nudged her sunglasses further up the bridge of her nose.

Tara glanced at her and shifted gears. 'Oh Ange. It'll happen for you, I know it.'

'Maybe.'

Ange's baby was a tiny wrinkled thing who died on the day he was born. He was buried in the backyard – straight into the earth, the way local custom dictated – the flat rock marking his grave. Ange wondered what he looked like now, the earth having worked on his body for a year. She sighed and clenched her fist around the seatbelt that dangled, unfastened, by her side.

Tara took the gravel path down to the beach and parked on the sand, where dogs lay on the shore, their ribs rising and falling with shallow breaths.

'Here,' Tara said, and passed Ange a pair of gloves, 'put these on.'

The gloves were long and thick – the sort of thing a farmer might use for wrenching a calf from the womb. 'Bit hot for this get-up, isn't it?' Ange dangled a glove by the rubber finger.

'Better than catching rabies,' Tara said, pulling hers on.

'Ok – I'm convinced.'

The women got out of the truck, each holding out a cow bone, and the dogs roused themselves.

'Come get it,' Ange said, backing towards the van. The dogs followed her, their eyes darting between the bone and the other dogs. When they got close to the truck, Ange threw the bone inside. One of the dogs jumped up and Ange grabbed its bottom half, shoving it in. She and Tara worked together, loading the wriggling, scratching dogs into the back of the truck. Sweat pooled under Ange's arms and between her breasts.

Inside the truck came the sound of howling and claws scratching against metal. Tara picked some dog hairs off her shirt and patted the truck. 'Better get moving before a fight breaks out.'

'Wait,' Ange said. 'Let's get that one.'

A lone dog stood a few metres from the truck. Bigger than the others, its orange fur was worn as an old carpet. When it panted, it revealed a pink tongue mottled with black. 'Here boy, come get it,' Ange said, holding out a bone. The dog came so close that Ange could feel its clammy breath on her legs. It sniffed the bone, turned, and walked away.

Ange made a grab for the dog and it whipped around and scraped its teeth on her leg. 'Jesus!' Ange said. There was a thin red line on her calf, but no blood was drawn. She lurched at the dog again but it scuttled to the shore where it sat by the waves, watching.

The school assembly area smelt of antiseptic and urine and fear. The mainland vets were positioned at steel operating tables, blue masks on their faces, performing operations on the knocked-out dogs. More dogs were locked in cages, where they whimpered and barked.

'What a day, I tell you,' the island vet said, raising her voice over the dogs. 'We're cutting and stitching for England. At this rate we'll be stuck here til midnight.'

Ange left Tara talking to the vet and wandered around the clinic until she found what she was looking for: a box of plastic ear tags. She looked around and slipped one in her pocket. There was no way she was doing that to her Ruby girl.

On the way back to town, Ange and Tara passed other volunteers loading dogs into trucks or carting them around in trolleys attached to scooters.

Tara pulled up near the butcher's, where a group of dogs had gathered. 'Easy targets,' she said. The women got out of the truck and the dogs circled them. One of the dogs had black fur, like Ruby, but with a white tip at the end of its tail.

'Aren't you a beauty,' Ange said, stroking under its chin. She went to the truck for some leftover chicken Tara had brought from her restaurant. When Ange returned, she saw the orange dog – the one who had nipped her at the beach – place its front legs on the black dog and start gyrating, its mottled tongue lolling out the side of its mouth. The black dog remained passive, as though a fly had landed on her back.

'Oh no you don't,' Ange said. '*Off!*' She shoved the orange dog and he made a strangling sound as he lost his grip and landed on the ground. Ange tried to grab him from behind, but he darted away. 'Bugger.' She knelt down to pat the black dog, its fur warm against her hands.

'Forget it,' Tara said, looking at the orange dog. 'He'll get his.'

Ange lost track of how many dogs she and Tara caught, how many trips they made to and from the school. By the time they stopped working, the sun's rays had lost their harsh edge and it was cooler, but still light.

Tara drove the truck back to her bungalow in the jungle, where Ange had left her scooter. 'Shall we have a drink?' Tara said. 'Unwind?'

In the distance, Ange could make out Tara's husband approaching. If he started talking, she'd be stuck here.

'Best be off,' she said. She wanted to get home quickly in case Maphit was still out. Ever since the accident, Ruby got skittish if she was home alone at night. The last time Ange and Maphit went to the mainland together, they returned after dark to find Ruby had chewed a hole in a flyscreen door and shat on one of Maphit's paintings. It had been all Ange could do to stop him from driving Ruby to the far end of the island and leaving her there.

In the light of the evening, the ocean was bleached a silver blue. Ange revved the scooter, willing it uphill. When she passed the uppermost point, she saw, emerging from the bushes, the orange dog. He stood by the side of the road, his eyes fixed on her. If only Tara was here with the truck. This time they would get him, she was sure.

The scooter gathered speed as it tipped downhill. When Ange was nearly level with the dog, he began walking, stopping right in her path. He looked at her, unflinching. Surely he would move. But the scooter got closer and still he didn't move.

Ange swerved. The scooter flipped over and skidded along the road, dragging her with it, before shooting out underneath.

She lay with her cheek to the asphalt, panting. It was the same feeling she had after being tumbled by a wave and didn't know which way was up. She placed a palm on the ground and looked to the sky, orienting herself. Her eyes swivelled back to earth, taking in the asphalt, the grass, the scooter. A few metres away, the orange dog looked on impassively, its mottled tongue nestled in its open jaw. Ange closed her eyes. When she opened them, the dog was gone.

The light had drained from the sky by the time Ange finished mopping the blood on her arms and legs with a sarong. The scooter didn't fare too badly: just a few scratches and a lopsided mirror. Ange rode home slowly, other scooters beeping as they passed.

When Ange pulled into her driveway and dismounted, she started shaking. She limped along the concrete veranda, one hand against the wall.

'Maphit,' she called. 'Ruby!' *Where were they?*

There was a bottle of rum on the veranda, near Maphit's painting gear. Ange sat on the outdoor couch and took a swig, savouring the heat in her throat. She closed her eyes. What she needed was rest.

There was a rumble in the garden and Ange woke, rubbed her eyes. A truck spluttered to stillness, its headlights glaring at the veranda. Maphit got out and walked towards her. There was something dark in his arms. Ruby.

Ange tried to stand, but her legs buckled underneath. She forced herself up again. 'What's going on?'

Maphit lowered Ruby to the couch. There was a rasp in his voice. 'She ran off – you know how she gets. It was dark, no one was here.'

'Is she…?'

'She's ok. One of the volunteers found her on the road to town. They took her to the clinic. That's where me and Uncle picked her up in the truck.' Maphit wiped his forehead with the back of his arm. 'I'm sorry Ange.'

'The clinic?' Ange saw the glint of white plastic stabbed in Ruby's ear. She moved her hand to Ruby's middle, felt the stitches along the length of her desolate belly. As she traced the ridge of skin between the stitches, she thought of the jar of flowers in the garden, of the roots that already were trying to take hold, spiralling inside the glass, demanding their place in the world.

Michael Bird

Michael Bird, born in Bristol, is an award-winning journalist and writer based in Bucharest. His short fiction has been published by Pulp.Net and he has been shortlisted for the Wells Festival of Literature Prize in 2011, the 2012 Hayward Gallery George Condo Prize and the 2013 Bristol Short Story Prize. He is winner of the 2015 Award for Best Initiatives of European Online Investigative Journalism (European University Institute, Florence, Italy). His work has appeared in multiple languages and been published in the *Independent on Sunday, Tagesspiegel, Design Week, New Statesman* and the *EU Observer.*

The Plait

Ana was the last name on the list. I had not met her at the court hearings or at the committee gatherings. Her name was not on any petitions. As far as I knew, the other women from the association did not speak to her. I never asked why.

Before the explosions, I used to see her at the end of the school day. She always stood several feet behind the school gates, away from the other parents. A tall and svelte figure, she had a taciturn demeanour that some took for arrogance.

Her daughter must have been about eight. She was a well-behaved, studious but happy child, who took Ana's hand whenever it was offered. She would pirouette, skip and run along the street, but was never more than a few steps from her mother.

The block where Ana lived was a rugged structure of naked concrete. In the corridor facing her apartment were pruned ferns, their pots moist, lying in a tray of shallow water. Her front door was varnished and well-maintained with a shiny spy-hole at the centre. I knocked, before seeing a bell stationed on the wall.

She opened the door in a pink flowery skirt, yellow blouse and heels. Around her neck were imitation pearls and she wore a subtle, flesh-coloured lipstick and a faint layer of rouge on her cheeks. Her hair was a strong and natural black.

"How can I help?" she asked.

"I'm sorry to disturb you," I said. "My name is Ion Ivanovich Ivanov. I am the father of Maria, from the school."

"Would you like to come inside?"

"That would be kind."

She led me through to the living room. The net curtains were drawn. In the corner by the window was a school desk, placed on top was an exercise book with a print of a tiger on its cover. A sharpened pencil lay alongside.

"Would you like to sit down?" she asked.

"Aren't you going somewhere?"

"I'm sorry?"

"You seem dressed up."

She covered her mouth as she laughed.

"In this town?"

To the left of the cemetery was a playground. On the side of a slide was a cartoon figure of a green dinosaur with white spots. Screwed to the frame of a pair of swings was the picture of a princess in a diamond-studded tiara. The ground was carpeted with broken pieces of wood-chip.

Next to the playground, the grass was clipped and lush. Each stone was bright, bold and wide, its marble glowing in the sunlight. Oval portraits of children and families were laid into the stone. In front were flowers, some fresh, others dry and black, set inside brass holders.

I had my own plot – four metres by two. A gift from the state. A rectangle of new-mown lawn.

A young woman was standing next to me in a black shirt and long pleated skirt, a grey band holding back her curly brown hair.

In her hand was a bunch of violets.

She separated them and held out a few to me.

"Would you…?" she asked.

"I have nowhere to put them," I said.

She leaned down over her daughter's grave, pulled some wilting stems out of the holder, laid them on the grass and replaced them with the violets.

In front of the stone, she bowed her head, stood for a few seconds, brushed her hands together and turned back to me.

"I'm Ludmilla's mother," she said.

"Maria's father," I said.

"Of course, Ion, I'm…"

"…Natasha."

"You'll want to talk to me, won't you?"

Ana perched on an armchair, her back straight, her hands on her thighs, as though she were unsure whether to stand up or relax. To her side, I sat on the sofa. It was deep and soft. When I leaned back, I felt I was reclining too far, so I pushed myself forward. My black bag was resting next to my hips. In front was a polished wooden coffee table, empty except for an ashtray.

"You live alone?" I asked.

"My husband works in Moscow."

"That must be hard."

"It's been seven years now."

"Does he come back often?"

"It depends what you mean by often."

I tried to ease back, but sank too far into the sofa, so I straightened up again.

"You have a job?" I asked.

"For the council."

"You're not on leave?"

"I prefer to work."

"I want to go back, but…"

"I like to be useful. I want to earn for myself, you understand? I don't like receiving something for no reason. It seems unfair. Like with these cars, you know? You see how many cars there are now?"

"In town?"

"Everyone has one of those jeeps. These wagons for transporting people over hills and fields. You know – the ones that are like tanks. From Japan or Germany."

"They're called SUVs."

"Everyone has an SUV," she said. "No one is working. Everyone is on leave. Yet they all have SUVs. What about you?"

"I was offered something like that from an official, I think, someone from the committee. It was at a meeting. He said there was so much money coming in, that we could all get a deal on a fleet."

"They jam up the roads. They fill up the car parks at the market. You can't move through the town. You can't move out of the town. Because every mother has an SUV."

It was three weeks after the incident. I was spending every day rushing between the hospital, the police HQ and a liaison office for parents in the mayor's office. There were many people who were supposed to be doing something for us – regional and national Governments and charities, plus men in smart shoes, polo-neck jumpers and leather jackets who appeared in our village. I solicited secretaries to make me appointments with any manager or deputy I could find. If my request was rejected, I stopped these officials in the street or outside the places where they worked.

One evening at the police station, close to midnight, one of the men in smart shoes and a leather jacket took me to a small room.

"Ion Ivanovich," he said, in gentle tones. "We are aware of your situation."

"Thank you. I would like to say that…"

"You don't need to say anything."

"But I want to make clear that…"

"What have I just stated?"

"That I don't need to say anything."

"And what are you doing now?"

I almost shouted.

"I am not getting any answers!"

"We know."

"So what else can I do?"

"Help."

"How?"

"By leaving the questions and answers to us."

I sat up for the rest of the night in my living room. A box of plastic toys in the corner. A row of picture albums on the lowest shelf of the bookcase. On the mantelpiece was a line of ceramic reindeer. The table was piled with paper from the last few days.

I could not eat. There was an impulse in me to head straight for the bottle, but I knew that drink would not help. Instead I spent the day lying on my back on the sofa, watching the sunlight ease shadows across the ceiling.

"They are not in the right order," a voice, distinct, familiar.

"What, what are not in the right order?" I was thinking aloud.

"The reindeer, Daddy, look."

"What order should they be in?"

"Petre should be first, then Victor."

"Which one's Petre?"

"You remember Daddy, you must remember."

"The pink one?"

"That's a girl reindeer!"

"But it has antlers."

"Oh Daddy, do you know nothing?"

A call. I stirred awake. It was six o'clock. I picked up the phone. A woman's voice told me I was requested in the mortuary.

I was seated with Natasha in a narrow kitchen. A plastic cloth patterned with orange and yellow flowers was spread across the table. On this lay a small loaf of bread on a wooden board. A pot of fish eggs to its side.

"I haven't prepared dinner," Natasha said.

"I'm not hungry."

"I usually make something."

"It's fine."

"Even if I don't have guests."

"It was spontaneous – my coming here. I wouldn't expect..."

"Honestly, with all this, I try to keep to a routine."

"I understand."

"That's what they tell us, isn't it? Keep to a routine, it will help. Do the same things every day. At the same time. Makes everything easier."

She poured the tea into two cups.

"My routine," I said, "is not to have a routine."

"I must remember that," she replied, picking up a small bowl from the kitchen side. "Sugar?"

"No thanks," I said, patting my belly. "Too much today already."

She placed the bowl back.

"What happened to your wife?" she asked.

"She died in childbirth."

"And her grandparents?"

"All gone – I've been mother, father and grandmother in one."

"Must have been tough."

"It wasn't," I said. "I was three people in love."

I sipped at the tea. It was warm, but lacked flavour.

Natasha gestured towards the bread and fish eggs.

"Please, help yourself, if you want some…"

"No," I said. "I will eat when I get home."

"But that means you're hungry."

"Much later," I said. "I will eat much later."

"If you change your mind."

"Thank you."

I looked down at my bag, leaning against the table leg closest to me, then raised up my head.

"I know what you're going to ask me," she said.

"It isn't good."

"Nothing is though, is it, anymore?"

"No."

"If it was, I would run from it."

The mortuary was only a few streets away from my apartment. My fingers were trembling. My heart was beating faster. As I left my block, my feet were numb and my head dizzy. I walked quickly, hoping the fast pace would calm me.

At the front door, a secretary buzzed me inside, led me downstairs and showed me into a freezing basement. At its centre was a giant metal slab, empty and clean. A white-haired doctor, stooping in a lab coat and smelling of tobacco, entered and greeted me.

"I'm sorry about the mess," he said.

I did not know what he meant. I looked down. Along three sides of the room were wide plastic boxes piled on top of one another. Inside lay frosted bags containing objects of different sizes – long, round, bulky and thin.

"Thank you for coming, Mr Ivanov," said the doctor. "As you know there was only one left unidentified. We have now ascertained the correct height and the dimensions of this person."

I could not see to what he was referring. I kept my head up, my gaze fixed on the doctor. Giddy, I rested my hand on the metal slab. It was cold. I pulled it away.

"It isn't Maria," he said.

"Then who is it?"

The trembling in my hands and arms accelerated. The face of the doctor began to blur. The room to shift its balance. There may have been anger – either concealed or obvious - in my voice.

The doctor took one step back.

"After the event," he said, "there was a lot of confusion."

Ana put her hands to her side, resting on the armchair and looked towards the window, down to the floor and back to me.

"Would you like a drink?" she asked.

"Do you know why I'm here?"

"I'm sure I have a beer somewhere."

"It's about your daughter."

"Oh," she said. "Her."

"I wanted to ask you…"

"I hope you didn't want to."

For some reason, I felt myself smiling.

"No, I didn't," I said.

"I'll get you that beer."

"Honestly, I'm fine."

"Please, no one else will drink it."

She went to the kitchen. I heard the opening and shutting of cupboard doors. I looked at the bookshelves. Translations of romance novels. Adventure stories. Their spines cracked.

"No, I was imagining things," she called to me. "I have no beer. I have vodka. Is it too early for you?"

"Really, I don't."

"Tea, I can do. But it will take a few minutes."

"Vodka is fine."

"Then I will join you."

A minute later she carried into the room a silver plate and a patterned cloth, bearing a half-full bottle and two upturned shot glasses.

"It's a nice home."

"It suffices."

I pointed to the window, where the exercise book with the tiger on the cover lay on a desk.

"I see you've left the…"

"Yes," she smiled. "I have a fondness for cats."

"But there are none here."

"This flat is not a place for such a creature."

She poured out small measures of the vodka and handed a glass to me. I was about to reach out my drinking arm towards her, but held back. The glass hung in my fingers.

"I've met with all the families," I said.

She looked at me with a sly, almost jealous glance.

"Why was I the last?"

"There is no reason."

"I wasn't important enough?"

Ana released a laugh, it was quick and loud and followed by a rasp. She put down the vodka and picked up a cigarette and lighter. Her nails were varnished in light pink.

Natasha had left the kitchen without telling me why. She came back holding a thick plastic album with a black and gold cover and a cardboard box for a pair of children's shoes.

She moved my tea to one side and put the album on the table. I was used to mothers showing me these. They were bulging, torn at the side, held together with tape and string. Inside were scraps of paper and cloth, small objects or icons, or a story revealing the girl's history, the funny things she did or those profound comments that children say by accident.

But not here. As I turned the pages, there were photographs, only photographs, stuck behind plastic sheeting.

A baby wrapped in a knitted blanket, its head and ears covered in a white cloth, lying on a double duvet.

A man in a cream turtleneck sweater, a cigarette in his mouth, holding the plump newborn in his hands.

Natasha laughing, the girl on her lap, her eyes snapped shut in the flashlight.

The inside of a church. A bearded priest in a black cassock and a yellow mantle. A series of pictures of the baby as the priest submerges her in a golden bowl. Her limbs shivering. Tightening in the cool air. The toes curling. Resisting the plunge. Kicking up the water. Her face shrieking. All out of focus. The girl's body shaking so fiercely, the background invades her space.

I had learnt to use a certain speed when flicking through such pictures. To linger on each pose for about five to ten seconds. To turn the pages slowly. To listen and nod as the women explained who was in the photos and what they were doing. But I never had any questions. Because if I started asking what was going on, I would hear too many stories.

But Natasha did not talk. Nor did she look down at the photographs. Instead she remained opposite, watching me – the corners of my mouth, the lines around my eyes and cheeks.

Ludmilla standing at the top of a slide. A pink anorak with a hood pulled around her face, covering her ears. Her hands on either side of the slide. Two knitted gloves tied to her wrists hanging free.

In a white cotton dress, she was seated on the knee of a middle-aged woman in a garden. A broken wheelbarrow lay half-submerged in the dirt behind. Above were plum trees, heavy with fruit.

A colour photograph of Ludmilla in the living room of what I guessed was this flat. It seemed to be the first day of school. She had a tiny-toothed grin and two black pigtails, a blue and white uniform and bright red heels. A skipping rope was in one of her hands and a small bunch of flowers in the other.

I knew the route to the school from here. I had passed by many times. The bushes, lawns and small fences at the side of the blocks. It seemed that every ten paces or so, Natasha had taken another shot of her daughter. Next to the bus stop, her face bright, alert, her stance in a rigid pose. Another from behind, her fuzzy body running down the main street, her heels in the air. The corner market. Blackcurrants. Blackberries. Pomegranates. Watermelons. Grapes. Piled up in wooden boxes. The girl standing in front. Another picture of her body running, from the side, beside a kiosk selling cigarettes and fake designer perfumes. In front of the school gates. A mass of other children, dressed in clean clothes, perfectly ironed, milling around with bouquets in their hands.

Ludmilla stands still among them, looking up at the camera. Another, where she retains the same pose, while a hand, flat, moves in front of the lens, reaching out, large and blurred.

"A few weeks afterwards, I wanted to clean," said Natasha. "I wanted to clean properly. I put all the books and all the crockery in boxes. I took out the furniture. Placed it in the yard. Hosed it down and dried it with towels. I turned up the carpets, hung them outside and beat them until I freed every speck of dirt. The rooms were bare, but needed sweeping. I brushed up and emptied the dust, nail clippings, seeds and hair into a bowl. We both had similar kind of hair. Hers was a little curlier and she wore it longer, but only by a few inches."

She closed the photo album and pushed it to one side, before placing the cardboard box in front of me.

"I sat on the living room floor. I laid out a piece of newspaper. I separated every strand from the dust. But when I collected them together, I wasn't sure which was my hair and which was hers. I washed and combed them and there was enough to twist into this."

She opened the top of the box. Inside on white paper wrapping was a thin braid of hair, about twenty centimetres long, with bands tied at either end.

"You know there is another child," I said. "A girl in the place where..."

"Please, don't talk about this."

"It is possible that…"

I always waited for a moment deep into the conversation before I unzipped my bag. Inside was a board with a metal fastener holding sheets of crumpled paper. Attached to this clip was a piece of string knotted around a pen. The thread was frayed and greyish brown from damp and sweat.

On the pages lay the smudged names and signatures of women.

"I don't believe what you're asking mc to do," she said.

"I understand."

"You've been there. You've been there with me."

"Yes."

"I offered you violets."

Ana leaned back, inhaled a long drag on her cigarette and moved her arm to one side.

"You want me to dig her up?" she said.

"There were clerical errors."

"What if it isn't yours?"

"We need to know."

"What if we have to do this to every child?"

"I want to be sure."

"Does it help us?"

"Isn't it important to be right?"

She crushed the cigarette out in the ashtray and looked over to the desk.

"Maybe I should open the curtains," she said.

I unzipped my bag and pulled out the clipboard. The pen still attached by string. I left it on the table.

Ana turned to me.

"No."

She spoke casually, as though pushing away someone in the street who had asked her for money.

"But," I said, "everyone has signed."

"Let me give you a suggestion instead."

"It's necessary, for you and for me."

"Ion Ivanovich," she said. "Does she still talk to you?'

"Yes."

"Is that scary?"

"No."

"It should be."

"I know she's safe."

"When you had guests around the house, before all this. They would crowd into your flat wouldn't they? Probably most of them in the kitchen."

"I guess so."

"And you wanted to talk to them. About what they were doing. Whose parents were in hospital. The funny things that had happened. The stupid things that people said. Who was working where and so on, yes?"

"Yes."

"And Maria would be there, wouldn't she? Playing around. With her dolls or her plastic animals, and she would notice you had guests?"

I nodded.

"And she wouldn't like it, would she? She'd come up to you all the time, pulling on your hand. Saying, Daddy, Daddy, come. Daddy, I want to show you something. Daddy, please."

"She did, yes."

"And what would you say to her?"

"I'd say, not now. I'm busy."

"And if she kept on insisting, and if she raised her voice?"

"I would tell her to shut up."

"So now, give her the respect she deserves."

"What do you mean?"

"Do the same."

Lisa K Buchanan

Lisa K. Buchanan has contributed fiction and essays to *The Missouri Review, Narrative, New Letters*, and *The Rumpus*. She lives and teaches in San Francisco. www.lisakbuchanan.com.

A Tough New Policy at the Food Pantry

Used to be I could recite some psalms or proverbs and leave with my cranberry jelly. Now you say I have to tell a story that *means* something to me personally. No more naked nymph with the saucy snake, no more arking up the quadrupeds for the deluge. Fine. You want resonance? I got resonance.

A man had two wives. First, the favorite, had shiny curls that bounced when she walked. As a girl, she went to exclusive private schools where she performed lines from Euripides, competed in chess tournaments, and made copper bracelets in Metal Shop for Girls. She did not fill out financial aid forms; did not widen the holes in her tights to make them seem intentional. Rather, she traded the prettiest clothes with the prettiest friends, and enjoyed the tastiest nanny-packed lunches. A walking superlative, she was never second in anything.

Second, however, spent her childhood with a widowed father who used words like "fellowship" and kept his family of two wandering from one sprawling chainstore nirvana to another in search of the perfect congregation. Or valet job. Or order fulfillment position. Ever the new girl, she became an expert at befriending her knee socks.

Now, First was married young to her godmother's eldest son. She never grocery shopped alone at night, lugging the bags up two flights of stairs into a dark, empty flat only to rush out again because she thought she heard a noise. Never took the garbage out Tuesday after Tuesday even when she had the flu, head spinning like a globe with melting polar caps. Never filched shiitake ravioli from her employer's refrigerator. And had certainly never been compelled to expound on scripture after standing in line to obtain canned green beans from a trailer in a church parking lot.

Look, wouldn't you like me to tell a happier story? Because this one about two wives, one loved and one unloved, might be a downer right before lunch.

First and her husband loved to take evening walks in their affluent neighborhood. Dawdling and smooching on one such unseasonably balmy occasion, the pair held hands and took up most of the sidewalk, oblivious to the possibility that the combined width of their bodies, though individually slim and strength-trained, might be an obstruction for less fortunate persons, such as the catering assistant who, still smarting from her supervisor's remark on the imperfect edges of her spinach triangles that day, had jumped off the bus a few stops early to avoid her own bleak block just a little bit longer.

The assistant found herself behind her clients by coincidence, but it was more than idle curiosity that compelled her to follow the couple at whose lavish annual holiday parties – three of them by now – she had served roast duck with cranberry chutney and passed trays of prosciutto-wrapped dates stuffed with chèvre. While the husband went into the ice cream shop, First stayed outside, dimpling her grin in an animated phone conversation. At a distance, Second (as she had already begun to call herself) stopped to view her father's text message about being fired by "another heartless Philistine." Eventually, the husband emerged with a cone in each hand. Bypassing

First, he headed straight for Second, confessing that not only did he remember her as the cute catering assistant who had worked his holiday parties, but that he wasn't sure whether it was the sultry night melting his Rocky Road or the sultry sight melting his resistance. "I couldn't forget you either," Second was about to say, when she was rudely jostled from her fantasy by a television news videographer nabbing footage of First and her husband as they traded flavored licks, wrists entwined.

When the couple resumed their stroll, Second followed with renewed purchase on two matters of import: how to keep her sad and sermonizing father from visiting during the holidays, and how best to maximize the cosmic misfortune that soiled the beautiful couple's otherwise immaculate life: First was barren.

This year once again, on the night of the party, it was Second's lot to wrap a garland of pine boughs around the staircase banister and string the front window with festive multi-faith lights. It was First's lot to descend those garlanded stairs in the glow of said lights, flutter her fingers, and hold sophisticated conversations about Vermeer or string theory or Peruvian pottery – never a dull slog about a catering assistant who worked fifty hours a week, had earned one third of a certificate in culinary management, and still owed $27,726.41 in student loans.

That's right, ma'am, serving up the personal, here and now in line at the Food Pantry. Pop-top tuna and add-water mash coming my way soon, yes?

And so. The couple's three-story home displayed numerous mosaic bowls, hand-crafted by First. Critics lauded them as "luminous," but Second saw them as emblematic of their maker – fragile vessels, decorative but empty. With no motivation other than kindness, mind, Second took care, during the festivities, to store the showiest pieces in cabinets and cupboards out of harm's way. Remembering that First had gone to bed early at previous parties, Second lingered by the punch bowl this time after the guests had departed. There, she found a way to mention to the husband (without revealing her knowledge of the couple's quiet search for a surrogate) that she had carried a baby to term for an egg-deprived cousin.

A few months later, after the tests and procedures and the negotiation of a payment more handsome than Second could have imagined, she was inseminated in a doctor's office. When Second had her morning sickness at night, the husband increased her surrogate pay to cover the catering shifts she missed. When she began to show and was relegated to the caterer's kitchen, he followed with another increase to replace her tip income. When she sprained her ankle, she didn't have to ask the beautiful (but anxious) couple to convert their sewing room to a guest room, drive her to her obstetrics appointments, and pay her bills.

Second put up with First's inquiries about the date of her last cigarette. First put up with Second's daytime talk shows. The latter kept her "second-but-fecund" affirmation private, even after overhearing First describe her as having been "leased like a goat for her kid-filled womb and milk-producing teats." Second hosted expectant-mom groups in First's living room, facilitating impassioned debates on cesareans and episiotomies, and wowing the gals with her spinach triangles (now perfected). First retreated to her studio to work on her bowls; the bowls she might have to abandon when the baby came; the baby she wasn't sure she still wanted.

The next holiday party would come eleven weeks before the baby was due. First insisted that she was up to the task, despite a slew of crippling migraines, but Second insisted that planning the party was the least she could do for her generous hosts. First wouldn't hear of it, adding that Second should not feel obligated to attend a function where, after all, she wouldn't know anyone. To the contrary, Second cited names from the guest lists she had archived and annotated, protesting that she wouldn't miss it for the world. The husband said that the planning would be stressful for

First. Second said that the idle weeks would be bad for the baby. First relented.

While First spent her days vomiting in a darkened bedroom, Second planned the party and became a demanding customer of the catering company where she had once been the scullion. She also planned the nursery, and was careful not to bother First with troublesome decisions about fabrics and crib design and limits on the household credit card. When Second was kind enough to wait until she found the husband alone before placing his palms on her belly to share the novelty of a fetal kick, First accused her of skulking, and complained, furthermore, that Second dressed to draw attention to her increasingly buoyant breasts. When the husband brought home two cashmere shawls identical but for color, Second curled up in hers while First lobbed her own into the giftbag whence it came – even though Second had offered to trade. Why, at one point, The Empty Vessel grew so obstreperous and paranoid as to insist that, in the television newsclip in which she and her husband had shared ice cream cones one balmy night the previous year, the bystander lurking off to the side under an improvised head scarf was Second. In short, First could not be pleased.

Look, I warned you that my story was not about restorething my soul or standething like wisdom on a mountaintop. And while I cannot promise that justice will prevail, I do think you'll find that my tale is not wholly bereft of happiness. Shall I continue?

Alone in the baby room, Second cradled a pillow in her arms, and privately rehearsed the how-we-met story that was bound, in her mind, to come in handy when chatting with the other mothers at school meetings and future holiday parties, long after the eternal menstruant would have slunk away in shame. "Most people date, marry, and have kids," Second told the mirror. "But he and I, we had our babies first…"

The dad-to-be was in excellent spirits. Not quite old enough to be Second's father, he was mindful when he walked next to her on the street, of the near salute she seemed to earn him from his fellow man, their gaze darting down to her rounded belly and then up to him who had caused it. It wasn't about whether he had burdened or fulfilled, impoverished or enriched, captured or protected. Rather, the point was that of abundance; his seed hath been made to multiply as the stars of heaven; greatness shall come forth out of his loins.

Okay, okay, forget the King James diction and cut to the fall of the mighty, right?

It did not happen at the holiday party, where revelers mazel tov-ed my taut, expectant womb; where eager aunts piled high the gift table and inquired about silver nitrate and cord clamping; where the husband dropped a honeyed fig slice onto my tongue, prompting the outgoing wife to go out indeed though the front door and run headlong into a certain gray-haired parking valet with a wrinkled red vest and more than one sad story about the heartless philistines of this world.

No, mine was a tedious, incremental demise. A few weeks before I was to deliver, I overheard First reserve a moving van. She then went on a buying spree – clothes, shoes, photography equipment, even a gigantic luxury vehicle to replace the low-emission compact of which she had been proud. First also resumed wearing makeup and meeting friends for lunch; leave she would, but with her head held high. The husband saw through this veneer of courage and, in an admirable display of sympathy, sought to temper her humiliation by tempering his affections for me. I bore this patiently. As much as I yearned to help First pack, as much as I wanted to wish her well and preserve our small remnant of cordiality, as much as I winced about the visible exodus of funds for her final farewell, I kept a respectful distance and pitied the marriage its death rattle. After all, I could afford to be magnanimous. Soon, the feeble life support of First's seniority would be unplugged, and I would lay a crisp, white sheet over its brow.

My weekend retreat on natural birthing was a luxurious gift, hastily presented, no doubt, to facilitate First's moving-out day. On my way back, blissy and self-assured, I bided my time at a home store, collecting tile samples for the imminent bathroom remodel. When at last I pulled into the empty driveway of the place I would soon call home, I took my time further still, pausing at the threshold in preparation for the lovely sight: no more shabby antiques and Persian rugs, no more sinky couches in dark chenille; and among the greatest mercies, no more "artisan" bowls cluttering up the coffee tables and backlit china cabinets.

But instead of the blank domestic canvas I had anticipated, the house sung First as it always had and I was greeted by a shock of items newly crowding my small room. Soft pink pillows had been returned to their plastic zipper bags, along with the rest of the spring-themed linens I had lovingly selected for the nursery. The hamper was filled with baby gifts from the holiday party, including a felt pond's five plush ducklings, now upended. To the extent that my bulk allowed, I rushed upstairs. The nursery had been redone in boyish blues and imperial gold. A low table hosted a model castle; the toy chest was stuffed with brainiac baby games. A globe-themed pillow would teach this child to hold the world in his hands from his crib days forward. A bright, new choo-choo chugged rhythmically around the plate-rail overhead, its high-pitched whistle mocking the scream I held in my throat. Nobody had to tell me that this room now awaited a child more cherished, more exalted, more worshipped than the one I would birth.

I collapsed into the nursing rocker. Had not the father of my child held my chin in his tender hands? Had he not lamented First's futile quest for maternity? Had he not deemed his progeny in my belly a rightful entrustment issued from the highest authority? Had he not proclaimed that the inferior present was stepping aside in deference to our superior future? And had not First wailed at him, amid a dramatic exit up the stairs, that something vital between them was missing? That some divine displeasure – an ancestral sin or neglected edict or a caution of nature – had rendered them childless? Had she not said that her immense sorrow would be daily exacerbated by having to raise the child of another woman's womb?

Furthermore, I was certain that their union was no longer carnal. No lust could have survived that efficient cheer that marked their daylight errands. Their kisses were chaste, fish lips puckering. They held hands like school chums skipping down the lane. They bantered in a juvenile made-up language of syllables known only to each other. With a domestic staff to handle the administration as well as the scutwork, the two of them did not so much run a household as they did play house. Never had I allowed myself to sleep until I heard the his-and-her doors close for the night on the pajama-clad spouses separately ensconced. It is unimaginable that I could have soundly snored while, directly above me, one lonely insomniac entered the private chamber of the other. Not after he had smoldered over me with stifled longing. Not after he had pulled me from a hallway into a darkened room just twenty feet from the movie-watching mosaicist, and ("Connie, O Connie") pressed his lips to my neck. Not after I had bought new sheets in preparation for our first night in his bed, and not, certainly not, while I window-shopped for engagement jewelry.

But there in the nursery, the soldier clock chimed, and the choo-choo clacked and whirred in an infinite loop. I, the fertile handmaid, had been put to immediate utility, while First had been primed for the miraculous. I would be whore and she would be holy; I would be soiled and she, immaculate; I would be crowned with broken twigs, and she, wreathed with fragrant jasmine. Second might furnish offspring for cheap labor, but it was First who would beget royalty.

I spent the final weeks of my pregnancy in bed with the capsized ducklings. As I grew heavier and wearier, my rival became light-hearted. While her pale pallor turned beatific, I scratched my thighs raw from prenatal eczema. The officious sounds of baby-proofing rang in my ears like a town crier. A stack of brunch invitations appeared on the hall table, heralding the imminent arrival of "our little man."

How then would it be for my girl to grow up as the playmate and servant of a young master, to test grocery-store cantaloupes for ripeness while he was tutored in philosophy, to pull his fermented boots off of him after his polo matches and return them aired and polished, to eat his leftovers alone in the kitchen and then scrub the plates? Would she, too, be pleasing and nubile and called upon, if not to yield fruit then simply to yield?

One day while I pretended to be napping, First wheeled the sewing machine into my room where it had lived before my arrival. The husband, whispering in the hallway, asked her whether that possibly could have waited. First murmured a sharp reply, adding that no, she would not retain "the hired uterus" in place of the cook who had retired.

"The transition for the child," he pleaded.

"The transition for you," she spat back.

Years and miles now from all of that, my family of two wanders. We line up at the food pantry with tale on tongue-tip. We load our dark sofas onto pick-up trucks and transfer my daughter's smiling bunny curtains, long outgrown, from one rented window-frame to the next. Once from a distance, I saw the beamy parents with their progeny. First was still elegantly dressed, her husband was still handsome, and their princely young son followed suit. But I was curious about the lass holding a baby.

A niece? A nanny? Or was it, perhaps, Third? Still, I hold fast to the belief that from my years of chaos, a kind of perfection will emerge. Like gods and mothers before me, I had filled my most wakingest dream with a universe conceived in my own image, both the ruin and the renewal, in the hopes that maybe someday, there'd be another chance for me after all.

Gina Challen

Gina Challen is originally from London, and moved to West Sussex in 1979. Whilst working as an Insurance Broker, she began a BA (Hons) in English and Creative Writing at the University of Chichester. In 2012, she left her job to complete a Masters Degree in Creative Writing. This she fondly calls her mid-life crisis. Her short stories can be found in anthologies published by Cinnamon Press, *Willesden Herald* and Rattle Tales, and have been read at the Shoreham Wordfest. Her critical essays are published online at Thresholds Short Story Forum. She can be found at www.ginachallen.co.uk.

Magpie

He feels as if he's always lived here, tucked away in the fold of the Downs, with the bulk of the hillside behind him. To the south, farmland stretches across the coastal plain, wrapping itself around the towns and parishes, before giving way to the sea. On a clear day, when he stands on the top of the hill, he can see the Isle of Wight. It shifts and shimmers in the light, as if it's floating, out there, on the distant horizon. But, when the cloud is low, mist rolls out across the fields, hiding the village under a thick, damp, blanket.

He doesn't have a steady job. When he's needed, he labours on neighbouring farms. He works with the seasons, coppicing in winter, lambing in spring, and harvesting in summer. He cleans ditches, cuts back hedgerows, and keeps footpaths open. In the autumn, he forages in the woods for cauliflower fungus. He carries a stick made from a twist of hazel. The wood at the top is smooth from years of handling and feels warm against his fingers. He uses the stick to poke around the base of pine trees, pushing back brambles to reveal the fungi. With a short-bladed knife, he'll cut the branching stems and lift the sweet, creamy mass.

When he works, he wears a brown jacket. It's old and discoloured. Stains spreading across the fabric like lichen on the bark of a tree. If the weather's too hot for a coat, he carries a canvas game bag strung across his chest. He was christened Jacob, but, as a small boy, his grandma called him Magpie.

The village is the only home he's known, but he wasn't born here; he's a *furriner*, brought down from London as a baby. While he's growing up, he understands this makes a difference. Besides, he's heard the stories of his mother's disgrace, and the gossip about her mini-skirted ways, the whispers of the adults repeated in the taunts of older children: *You're a come-by-chance, and y'mum's mawky. She's a slut, and that's no better than she should be.*

Each year, on his birthday, a card arrives in the post. He places it in an alcove of the fireplace, next to a china shepherdess. The picture of a carefree Mickey Mouse, with his red shorts and yellow shoes, stands out like a blemish against the dull brickwork. If he's lucky, he finds a fold of dollar bills caught in a paper clip and secured beneath the greeting. He keeps them, still folded, in a tin under his bed, along with the envelopes the cards came in. After his sixteenth birthday the cards stop arriving.

His mum is bound to come back for him when she's settled, his granny tells him. Or perhaps she'll send for them both, and they'll have an adventure going across the sea to live with her. Try as he might, he can't imagine his granny ever leaving the village, but the year he's thirty-five and she's eighty-three, she leaves him. People said that she'd made old bones.

He keeps the cottage the same as it's always been, coats hung on the pegs inside the back door, boots and bags jumbled in the corner, fungi in nets, dangling above the Aga to dry. His grandma's clothes are still hanging in the wardrobe. Now he's alone, he likes to read. He picks westerns, biographies, and whodunits, buying at random from church fetes. There's something comforting in owning these fragments of other peoples' lives. Once a fortnight, from the library van, he orders books on far off places, and memorises facts. He reads about the pioneers, who left carrying their homes in wagon trains. He reads about explorers and travellers, and about nomads and gypsies. He likes to read about people who've journeyed across rivers and mountains, searching for a different life.

Fridays, if he has cash, he drinks cider in the pub, leaning against the bar with his friends. He's grown up with these men, sitting next to them in school, working beside them on the land. Now they're older they call him Mag. They talk about football and the cost of the Olympics. They argue about culling badgers, trade stories about Foot and Mouth, and worry about the threat of a new virus devastating the flocks. They no longer remember the belongings that went missing from their desks. Yet, he can still see them in the playground, yelling, *Magpie's a fucking spazz*, when they spilled the hoard he'd gathered from his raided rucksack. He's never forgotten the sudden pounding in his chest, or how tears lurched from behind his eyes, while he stood, head bowed, in a rain of sweets, pencils, and loose change.

When he walks around the village, he finds things. He knows how to look. He picks up old tickets and odd coins by the bus stop, a pen in the porch of the village hall, and cigarette butts smudged with lipstick from outside the shop. Later, back at the cottage, he places them safely amongst his collections. Sometimes, while he waits in the farm office, he slips his hand into the pockets of unguarded coats, and his fingers search amongst creased tissues for hidden treasures.

In the lambing sheds, he takes the night watch, moving easily amongst the ewes, pulling newborns free, and wiping mucus from their mouths. He clears the placenta into buckets for burning, and sprinkles antiseptic powder across the fresh straw. It's warm inside, the air heavy with the breath of a hundred animals and the acrid smell of urine and blood. It's not unpleasant, but still he drinks his coffee outside in the clean, cold air, watching for the dawn.

There's a woman working in the shop he speaks to. She's new to the village, and in the pub there's talk about her, where she's come from, and why she's here. She always smiles at him when he buys his paper. They chat together. They discuss the weather, television programmes, how to stop smoking, and what they'll cook for dinner. He likes the way she knots a scarf around her neck, and how her hair shifts and shines under the lights as she moves behind the counter. He sees the tight pull of her jeans as she bends to stack the shelves. When he can, he helps her close the shop, putting out the rubbish, breaking down the empty boxes, and sweeping the floor. He waits while she cashes up the till, and walks her home.

He talks to her about his work on the hillsides, and about the books he's reading. One afternoon, he places a feather from the wing of a green woodpecker on the counter. He tells her how he found it outside the school. How he spotted it lying against the railings, amongst the dead leaves. She picks it up. "Funny, it looks yellow in the light." And she traces the colour with her finger tip.

"So pretty," he says. Then he tells her about the woods and how he looks for the cauliflower fungus.

"I found my stick leaning up against the wall in the porch of the church."

"Somebody must have lost it. I'm surprised they didn't come back for it, aren't you?"

"I don't know. I wanted a good stick."

"Okay, I see."

Later, when he is helping her tidy up, she says, "It must be fun, foraging."

"We'll go in the autumn," he says. And he puts his arm around her shoulders. She jerks away, telling him she'll be much too busy to go.

"And I'm in a rush, tonight," she says. "I've got a date. A film, then dinner. Why don't you go, I can manage here. Really, I can. You go." She looks straight into his face. He can see the rigid tendons in her neck, the gloss of her lipstick. "Please, go."

He stands for a moment, his hands on his thighs, his fingers splayed, as if he is holding himself upright.

"Please," she says. Her voice is a whisper.

As he lets himself out through the back door in the store room, he spots her scarf, draped across a chair. He lifts it to his face, and brushes the cool, silky material against his lips. He slips the scarf into his pocket.

He spends the end of summer mending fencing and stiles. His pickup is loaded with posts and planks, and he travels across the farmland, from site to site. It's hard work, digging out rotten posts and bedding in the new, pulling taut the strands of wire and securing them with metal staples to the wooden posts. He'll be paid a day rate. He keeps a tally in his notebook: Glatting Hanger – eight days. Pitchurst Copse – six days. He always adds an extra day.

They come in the early morning when he is working his way down through Left Hanger, repairing the fence between the fields and the edge of the forest. There are four joggers, all women, legs outlined in black lycra and water bottles in their hands. He stands aside, amongst a tumble of bramble and faded cow parsley, to let them go by. The last runner has dark hair pulled back from her face.

"Morning," she says. And he sees the swing of her hips, and the muscles in her thighs. His hands feel hot inside his heavy leather work gloves. She leaves a faint scent of honeysuckle behind.

The next day, he leaves his fencing, to search for signs of cauliflower fungi. It's early September and they've only just begun to grow. He probes around the scrub beneath the pines, noting the position of the fruits for later. It doesn't occur to him that the joggers may return, and, as he goes back through the wood to his work, he's surprised by the dull beat of their running. He crouches down. Through the dried heads of cow parsley and old man's beard, he spies the joggers moving along the footpath. The woman pauses, jogging on the spot. She gulps water from her bottle, and he sees the pale, secret hollow under her arm. He waits, motionless amongst the undergrowth, until her footsteps are echoes on the chalk.

It takes him three weeks to finish this job, working along the fence line, chopping back the undergrowth as he goes. He continues through the weekends. Each morning, cutting and hammering his way down the footpath, he watches for the runners. As he works, he thinks of how, tomorrow, he'll speak to her. Conversations form, disperse, and reform, until all the words they could use fill his head.

In the evenings, he finds he can't read. He drops the paperback on the floor by his chair, no longer caring about the drama played out in the pages. Library books remain unopened, stacked on the table. He thinks about the woman running through the woods, wonders how it would be if he took her to the pub for a drink. She'd be dressed in jeans and a soft white t-shirt. He calls her Claire. He imagines her hair shifting across her shoulders as she walks. He feels the tingles as it brushes across the back of his resting hand.

Come Monday, it will be time to move on to his next job. He lays awake, curled on his side, staring at the window. By six o'clock, although it's still dark, he parks his pickup at Toby's Stone. He begins to track back through the woods to Left Hanger, pushing the bracken and bramble aside with his stick. In the cold air, he catches the scent of fox, harsh and oily, and a movement stirs the undergrowth as he passes. The sun rises. He hunkers down beside a pine tree. In his old jacket, he's no more than a shadow on the ground. He thinks of the fungi, untouched beneath the scrub. If he cuts one today, it'll be the first he's taken this autumn.

He waits, watching the dawn light flame across the sky, until the familiar thud of trainers draws him, and he creeps, tree by tree towards the footpath. When the women have passed he emerges, tilting his head towards the breeze.

From his game bag, he lifts the cauliflower fungus, and carries it to the sink. The fruit is young; it's still milky white, the fragrance not yet matured. He should have left it to grow bigger, should have let it carry on pushing out lobes and collecting up the minute debris of the forest floor. He holds it under the tap, letting the running water rinse out a hoard of grit and pine needles.

Tonight, he'll fry the fungus, and make an omelette. He cracks three eggs into a bowl and beats them with a fork, piercing the membrane around the yolks, and whisking until the liquid froths a deep, pure yellow. With a twist of his wrist, he slides a knob of butter across the hot surface of the frying pan. While the butter melts, he takes a sharp knife and cuts through the flesh of the fungus, sliding the slices back into the sink. He uses his fingers to feel for any remaining cache of dirt.

When he touches a hard swelling deep within the lobes, he thinks he's found a small stone, buried in the soft fungal tissue. If he is right, he'll keep the stone in a box, with others he's found. As if he were shelling a bean, he draws his thumbnail across the top, and hooks the object free. An earring falls out, and comes to rest in his hand. Against his palm, three red stones, set in a gold mount, glisten like sparks from a fire. He drops it on the table, stepping back, as if he were in danger of being burnt. On the Aga, the searing butter hisses and spits in the pan. As it browns, it fills the kitchen with the bitter scent of charred cob nuts.

He sits at the kitchen table, drinking coffee, looking at the earring. He rolls it between his thumb and forefinger, feeling the rise of the gold against the faceted gems. He closes his fist around it and, holding it tight, picks up a library book. He reads of Native Americans riding across wide open plains, of hunters and gatherers, of necklaces made from carved stones, and of the willow hoop of the dream-catcher, that the shaman decorate with the findings of everyday life.

As the dark begins to fade, he wraps the earring in a cotton handkerchief he's taken from his grandma's room, and pushes it into the pocket of his jacket. He drives to Left Hanger, and leaves his pickup in a gateway. On foot, he follows the hedge line to where the footpath drops into the woods. Shielded amongst the hawthorn, he waits.

"Have you lost anything?" He steps forward as the first woman climbs the stile. Her dark hair's scraped into a ponytail, and there's a sheen of sweat across her forehead.

"Jesus Christ! I didn't see you." Behind her, the other women are jogging on the spot, their breath ragged in the damp morning air.

"I found this." He pulls the handkerchief from his pocket, uncovering the earring. With his palm outstretched, he offers it to her.

"Oh." She lets go of the upright post and steps away from him. He sees her teeth bite against her bottom lip. "It's not mine."

"It's for you. Please, take it." He smiles.

"Come back this side with us." Her friend reaches out to guide her.

Without turning away from him, the woman stretches back with her foot and pulls herself up onto the stile.

"It's not hers, alright." Her friends grab her hand, helping her down.

"Claire?" he says.

"Claire? You're mistaken, I'm not Claire. Sorry, it doesn't belong to any of us." She looks at her friends. "So, we need to go now, okay?"

The women edge away, pace by pace, until, as one, they begin to run, retracing their steps along the path.

Although it's not Friday, he goes to the pub. The fire's been lit and the bar smells of wood smoke. He drinks his cider quickly, throwing back his head, his Adam's apple chasing up and down. The glass rocks as he sets it on the bar and pushes it towards the landlord.

"Another, Mag? Christ, take it steady, mate. I'm not going t'run dry."

He joins a game of three hundred and one, aiming only for the bull's eye, throwing the darts so hard they ricochet off the wires. He chooses not to take part in any of the discussions and, when the conversation turns to women, he downs his pint and leaves.

Back at the cottage, he wanders from room to room, the earring held tight in his fist. In the kitchen, he unwinds a black bin liner from the roll, and carries it up to his bedroom. He kneels on the floor and pulls a tin out from under his bed. As he takes off the lid and tips the contents over his bed, the earring slips from his hand. It falls amongst the litter of birthday cards, envelopes, and dollar bills on to the duvet.

Florence Delaney

Florence Delaney lives with friends on the banks of the River Lee. She is a data analyst for kidney transplant research. She loves painting, peaches, blackbirds and the Cornish sea. She is writing a series of 22 stories, one for each card of the Tarot Major Arcana. *The High Priestess* and *The Hermit* have been published in the online magazine *Don't Do It*. This is the eighth card.

Justice

There were three of them. Three girls. The littlest girl was very little, but the middle girl and the eldest girl weren't so big either. Rose pink dresses spattered with mud and and lacy socks that had once been white. The patent leather of their shoes was scored and dusty.

"I can hear a dog," said the littlest girl, and the two bigger girls looked at each other, knowing what it meant. Policemen in heavy boots were hunting them across the mountain.

It was dark. Only the moon gave light. Harder to move in darkness, and now they were imagining the black-uniformed policemen moving swiftly, trained to be silent, gaining on them. The girls were untrained.

"Should we find somewhere to wait for morning?" asked the middle girl.

The eldest girl was thinking about scent. Everywhere they'd been they'd laid a line of scent, and now if the dogs came upon it they'd follow the line straight to them.

"We need to find a river," she said. "Listen out for water."

The eldest girl and the middle girl had done something bad and now the police were hunting them. They had done something bad and then tried to escape, which meant they were cowardly. They had tried to escape and taken the littlest girl with them, which meant they were reckless and selfish. The middle girl hadn't wanted to take the little one.

"Leave her behind," she said. "She's not in trouble."

But the eldest girl knew more. She knew that the littlest girl would be haunted her whole life by what the other girls had done. She knew there was no escaping it. She knew they had to get as far away as they could.

The littlest girl couldn't walk very far, so sometimes they carried her. Three girls in ribbon sashes. They moved slowly. They made for the woods and the mountain. They hid in a cellar for two days while a whole town looked for them. Then the trees began.

"I think I hear it," said the littlest girl. They all listened. Something: it might have been water running, but it might have been the wind in the pinebranches. They followed the sound. They heard the dogs bark again, and the barking's echo.

And there it was: a stream.

"We need to walk in the water," said the eldest girl. "That way the dogs won't find us."

They had made sure, on the first day, that the littlest girl knew not to cry. They had made quite sure. Now they helped her with the buckles to her shoes. They took her socks off and stuffed them into the toes. They carried her shoes for her, along with their own.

The littlest girl said, "This water's cold."

The middle girl took her hand and squeezed it. "It won't be forever. Just until we're sure the dogs can't catch us."

They followed the stream up the mountain. Ankle-deep. The water was so cold their feet burned; it felt like they were walking through fire. But the littlest girl did not cry.

The eldest girl knew it wouldn't work to walk up the stream forever. She knew the police dogs would follow their scent to the edge of the water, and as soon as they did the policemen would start to trace the path of the stream both uphill and downhill. Now they had to disappear into the forest.

"Here," she said. "Now we get back on land"

Their feet had gone numb and it was difficult to get their socks and shoes on. The littlest girl said, "Oh!"

"What is it?" asked the eldest girl.

"I don't know – worms, maybe –" said the littlest girl. There were three leeches on her left foot.

"Don't look," said the eldest girl. She and the middle girl picked them off and blood came out. They pulled her socks on and blood soaked into the socks. They did up the buckles on her shoes.

They were far up the mountain now, and now that they were on land the path was steep and the way uneven. Tree roots rose up out of the ground in great black waves.

"Like dragons' necks," said the middle girl.

They could still hear the dogs, but they were further off now. They found a place where the rock jutted out and hung over a patch of moss and fungi. They slept.

When they woke, the ground was soaked with dew. Dew had soaked into their dresses and hair where they lay on the ground. Their feet were still wet. They shivered.

The eldest girl was still thinking about the dogs. She was thinking that the dogs might smell the path they'd cut away from the stream. Ashes would cover the scent, but the ground was wet and everything was too damp to burn. Later. When the dew was dry.

They made a line around the mountain.

"How long now?" asked the littlest girl.

"Not long," said the eldest girl. "Don't keep asking."

The middle girl and the eldest girl had done a bad thing, but it wasn't fair to hold the middle girl responsible. She'd only done what the eldest girl had told her to do, and if she'd done more, well, the eldest girl hadn't stopped her. The eldest girl could have said, "Stop! Let's not run away. Let's admit we did it."

The middle girl might have done this. She didn't know what it meant to have such a thing hanging over you for the rest of your life. Only the eldest girl knew.

As they walked around the mountain, the eldest girl kept bending down to touch the twigs and moss. She wanted to know if they were dry enough to start a fire. Not yet. The trees were like narrow black lines rising up from the mountain. Even where the mountainside was steep, the trees still rose in a straight line, growing towards the sky. They were too covered in spiny branches to give shelter.

When the eldest girl thought about being found, she wanted to be dead. The others did not yet understand that some things were worse than dying. Only the eldest girl understood. She knew that after they were found, the other girls would wish they had died back on the mountain.

Only the eldest girl had known, when they did the bad thing, that there was no life after.

She reached down and the ground was dry. "Let's light a fire," she said. "Get moss and little sticks and big sticks."

"So we can get warm," said the middle girl.

"No," said the eldest girl. "For the ashes."

The fire was small, hard to keep going. The littlest girl ran back and forth with handfuls of sticks in her chubby fists. The eldest girl poked at it and the middle girl tried to fan it with dead tree branches.

They needed enough ash to cover themselves completely. It was the only way to escape the dogs.

It was lovely to watch the flames. Sheets of orange and white shimmered into and out of existence. The eldest girl knew about the secret fire that hovered above the visible flame, a place where the flame itself was colourless. It could be seen only as a little quivering in the air. The littlest girl splayed the fingers of her hands and stretched them towards the warmth. Her small palms were pink with heat.

They could have stayed there all day, but they were afraid to. They let the fire burn out.

The middle girl reached out to get a handful of white ash, but the eldest grabbed her wrist. The embers were still hot. They needed to wait until the cold set in.

"I'm hungry," said the littlest girl. "Are there any more biscuits?"

"No," said the middle girl. "We ate them all yesterday."

"Oh."

They had made sure she would not cry.

They rubbed ash up their arms and on their faces and over their feet. They rubbed it into their hair. The pinkness of their lips was grotesque. They rubbed ash onto their clothes. It was important to take away the scent. If they smelled like humans, the dogs would find them. They needed to smell only of burning.

The eldest girl picked up the littlest girl and they began to climb further up the mountain. The path was treacherous. Rocks that looked stable moved under their feet.

The littlest girl clung to the eldest girl's neck. She was small and perfect. Her knees were dimpled, and the hair on the back of her head still grew in baby curls. The eldest girl held her tight.

The eldest girl wondered whether it wouldn't be better to kill the little one. She was so small and trusting that it would be very easy. Now, while they had the chance.

The trees were starting to thin and the air was colder. Their cheeks prickled with it. Past the snowline was a long ridge where the one mountain met another, and another, and carried on until it was far away from anything. As the trees thinned they started to see the outline of it. A white line against the sky.

"We'll go there," said the eldest girl. A high walkway, leading – where? Somewhere else.

Somewhere nobody would know their faces, or what they had done.

The littlest girl chewed at the end of a stick. She never swallowed any, just sucked and gnawed at the end until it separated into woody strands.

"That's disgusting," said the middle girl.

The eldest girl looked at the hard rocks below them, and wondered.

They were getting cold, and it was slowing them down. They had been cold before, but this was a new kind, a creeping, damp mist in the air. They felt it in their sides and in their backs, where the muscles tensed and shivered but could not get warmer. They felt it inside them. It was worst for the littlest girl, because she was so small. And as the sun got lower, they got colder, and the trees thinned out enough to let a little of the wind through.

Something in the wind. A voice.

The eldest girl pressed the littlest girl to her shoulder and covered her ear, gently, as if she were keeping it out of the wind. But the littlest girl's eyes had gone big and she wriggled free. She lifted her head up and listened.

The voice, again. No words.

The little pink mouth half-open, the eyes white against soot-smeared cheeks. Like the snow against the grey rock.

And again. Closer, now, coming from below, where the trees were thicker. "Hello! Come back! I love you!"

The eldest girl hurried onward, higher. But the other two girls had heard. And then, "I know you didn't do it!"

The girls were too surprised to say anything. They stood there, listening for more. But there was no voice, only the wind.

Then something almost inaudible. And they started to walk again, without thinking. They needed to keep going. To be fast.

But the littlest girl whispered into the eldest girl's neck. Her voice was thick and strange.

"My mama."

It was a lie, and a terribly dangerous one. The idea that they could wipe the last few days away like yesterday's incorrect sums from a blackboard. Of course they wanted to believe it. And of course they couldn't. If they started to believe the lie, the cold and the hunger would slowly change from uncomfortable to unbearable. Like swimming in a place with a silent, dangerous current. They wouldn't notice the movement until they were already lost.

The littlest girl had dropped the stick and was sucking on two fingers. She was scared.

"Was it real?" she asked.

How far would a small person have to fall in order to die? Her skull would have to break as soon as she hit the rock. The middle girl couldn't know. She wouldn't understand. Make it look like an accident.

Maybe the eldest girl couldn't do it. Maybe she was too cowardly, and certainly, she was selfish. The small hand was cold in her hand. She had always found it hard to do the right thing.

The light lowered and turned purple and they neared the edge of the trees. A bitter wind cut their faces. It was flatter, here, and the snow was the only bright thing around.

"No more voices," said the middle girl. The others didn't say anything.

"Maybe they turned back," said the middle girl.

The littlest girl said, "The moon's here."

The moon was pink. They'd have to walk all night, because if they slept in the snow they'd never wake up. The eldest girl was so tired she didn't know what to do except keep walking.

And then, the voice again, from the thick, dark trees. "Are you there? I love you! Come back!"

The eldest girl stepped onto a patch of ice and fell.

She wasn't badly hurt. She'd just turned her ankle. It was painful, but nothing else was injured. Then when she stood on it, it hurt more.

"We'll have to go slower," said the middle girl. They started to climb up the slope, stepping carefully, the wind biting at them with sharp teeth.

"Please, please, come out!" called the mother's voice, rusty and strained.

The littlest girl said, "Oh, couldn't we –"

"Shush," said the middle girl quickly. "It's a trick."

The eldest girl said nothing. They were walking too slowly. They needed to get up onto the ridge as soon as they could, away from dogs and policemen and the voice and the forest. On the top of the ridge they would be unable to hear anything but the wind.

She tried to walk quickly, but the ankle gave way. Frightened as she was, she couldn't make herself put more weight on it. It took all the self-control she had to keep walking at all.

Maybe the foot would get numb as she got colder. Maybe she'd get a body of ice that felt no pain. Maybe they'd run across the ridge, the wind in their ears, and forget everything. Run over one mountain and then another. The eldest girl wished, intensely, that she had fallen just a little harder, onto a hard rock, into blackness. The moonlight spilled over the snow. She pulled at the sash around her middle, a thick pink ribbon.

And she could feel it, the slow, sad pull of the drifting current, pulling her feet from under her. She could imagine being tucked into a clean white bed, and kissed on the forehead for goodnight.

The voice was cracking. "Where are you? I won't hurt you. I know you didn't do it."

The middle girl stopped dead still and said, "Maybe –"

"You need to keep going," said the eldest girl. "You need to be fast."

The middle girl's eyes were big. "Couldn't we all –"

"No. You need to run as fast as you can."

It was harder for the eldest girl, moving downhill. Each step onto the ankle made her breath catch. She started to cry, quietly.

Then she called out, "Hello! I'm here!"

The trees were sparse shadows here. The mother came up the slope, a smaller shadow. She held her arms out wide.

The mother held the eldest girl tight against her body. Her hands in the eldest girl's ratty mass of hair. Her breathing. And the eldest girl, almost not breathing, because she was held so tight.

She wanted to know where the other girls were. Because they were all precious.

"It's too late," said the eldest girl. "They are far off. They left me behind." She showed the ankle where it was purple and swollen.

"They got away," said the eldest girl. "Not me."

The mother and the girl were climbing down the mountain together. They would walk until they found a road. The mother's clothes were smeared with soot where she had pressed the girl into her and held her there.

Now, though, she wasn't touching the girl. She did not offer to lift her or help her down the path, even though the girl was limping badly and sometimes let out little cries of pain. The mother walked a few feet away from her, watching her every step.

They were climbing down the mountain. The eldest girl looked around and wondered if she could fall again, if she could pretend to trip and let her body drop onto the rock. It would be difficult. The mother was watching her very closely. And what if she didn't die? It was harder than anyone might think, to die for certain.

She was cold to her very centre.

Then the eldest girl saw, through the black tree branches, two pairs of white eyes. The other two girls were following them.

They must have allowed themselves to doubt, in the cold wind of the mountain ridge. They must have felt the snow seep into their patent leather shoes. And so they had followed. They had watched the mother hold the girl to her chest so tight she could hardly breathe. Their hungry eyes had taken it all in.

The eldest girl felt despair for the first time. She had not been able to save them.

The mother did not help, but she didn't try to hurry the eldest girl along. And so they crept down, slowly. The stars moved across the dark sky. And from time to time the eldest girl saw a movement out of the corner of her eye.

"Where are we going?" she asked.

"To a road," said the mother.

She was tired, and cold, and in pain. Her stomach was empty and her head kept swimming. She had not saved them.

"It's all true, you know," said the eldest girl. "Everything they said. I knew it was wrong. And I knew it was wrong to take her with us, but we didn't think."

The mother kept walking in silence.

"Her life is ruined," said the eldest girl. "Both of their lives are ruined, because of me."

The mother was sweeping her hands over her clothes where the soot clung. She was trying to brush herself clean, but the soot was worked in.

The eldest girl could not be sure, on her own, of getting really dead. She couldn't even climb anywhere high; her ankle hurt too much.

"If they found me here," she said, "no one would know how I died. This is the last chance."

And she saw at last that the mother, too, was caught in a current. It would pull at her quietly, almost unnoticeably, until it drew her under.

"The last chance..." breathed the mother, so quietly.

The eldest girl said, "They are running over the ice. They left me behind because I got hurt. They are hard, now, and cold. They have to be. They will always be frightened. It will be behind them, always. They will dream of only this for ever."

The mother took the eldest girl by the shoulders. Her face was pale, and she was trembling. The eldest girl untied the sash from around her middle. She held it out in her two hands. She held it out without saying a word.

The mother's hands shook as she tied a knot in the pink ribbon sash. The eldest girl was frightened, but she was also ashamed. What the mother didn't know was that the eldest girl deserved worse than this. The eldest girl deserved to live for a long time. But the middle girl and the littlest girl needed to see that there was no undoing.

They needed to run. They had turned back, and so they would need to run very quickly to make up the lost distance. They would have to run as if a whole pack of dogs were at their back.

The mother placed the loop of the sash over the eldest girl's head. The eldest girl was worried, for an instant, that perhaps it would break; but it was a thick sash. And made from real silk, too; at least, that was what they had told the littlest girl.

The mother threw the end of the sash over a low branch, and pulled it tight. At first it cut into the eldest girl's neck. It hurt. It was frightening. Her face began to burn as the blood pooled into it. And then the silk was pushing, hard, against her windpipe. It was so hard to think of anything but the breath that would not come, even as she pulled it in with all the muscles of her chest and diaphragm. She looked frantically for faces in among the pines. They must see this. It couldn't be undone. The ribbon caught under her chin and she felt the forest floor drop. Her legs kicked of their own accord, trying to get hold of a ground that was falling away; and her eyes began to darken.

And she choked and choked, and the breath did not come. She heard somebody screaming, and understood with some surprise that it was the mother, that the mother was screaming. And there they were, in between two trees, a pair of white faces and pink dresses with ribbons tied in long bows at the back. Why didn't they run? They were watching. The black was seeping in from the edges of her vision, and she kicked and kicked, and did not ever truly stop hoping that the breath would come.

Chris Edwards-Pritchard

Chris Edwards-Pritchard is a 25-year-old writer living in Gloucestershire, UK. His work has been published in a range of anthologies and magazines, including New York journal the *Bellevue Literary Review*, and the *Irish Literary Review*. One of his stories has been considered for broadcast on BBC Radio 4, and last year, he was delighted to accept the Gregory Maguire Award for Short Fiction in London. This is the second time his work has appeared in the Bristol Short Story Prize Anthology. You can follow Chris on Twitter: @ChrisEPritchard.

Just After We Stopped Talking

There I am chucking scraps of our old kitchen into Wood when who do I spot parking up in front of Non-Recyclable? Helen Hawkes. Of all people. Blow me down. In the same old Citroen she's always driven. As if she's just popped across the border from The Distant Past. Like a crummy low budget version of that Marty McFly film. Can't remember the name. Paddy was watching it on Netflix the other day.

I get chatting to her. She tells me it's a pleasant surprise. And I say: ditto. We both think about hugging but neither initiates. I hold back due to sweating issues alone. You try hauling cupboard doors and bottoms of cabinets around in this heat without succumbing to a little perspiration.

I'm being serious.

And the smell.

We're at the Tip, but who knows if it's my armpits or the heaps of rubbish.

There are seagulls swarming overhead.

Though Paddy tells me there are no such thing as seagulls.

Just gulls.

It's been almost twelve years since I last saw Helen. She tells me about Clayton, but I already know about Clayton. I tell her that I saw something about it on Facebook the other day. This comes as a surprise. She nods a slow little nod. She clearly forgot that we watch each other's lives unfold on computer screens every day.

Or at least: I watch hers.

"Which one was that?" she says.

"A couple of days ago," I say. "A photo."

"That was probably Ken."

"A TimeHop I think, or whatever it's called?"

"I really hate those things," she says.

She screws up her face to show me just how much she hates them.

She has this small little face, framed by a ginger fringe. And just a smudge of eyebrow now. Two little smudges sitting high above the wrinkles, and the clotted eyelashes, and those terrifically alert peepers. She has aged only in as much as her face has become more tired. It is a more tired version of the face that I used to know.

It happens to everyone.

No biggie.

"It was a photo of all of you," I say. "The whole gang – Ken, Daisy, Gem, when they were little, and Clayton was there too but he'd been blacked out."

Ken, Daisy, Gem, Clayton.

My God – I haven't said those names out loud in a while.

But they came back quick enough.

The brain is a wonderful thing.

"Kenny's always posting things online," says Helen.

"They're all at it, Hells."

That's what I used to call her.

I touch her on the arm as I say it.

I used to do that too.

"Him especially," she says.

"You were at Butlins," I say.

"When?" she says.

"In the photo."

She pushes her bottom lip down with her top lip.

As in: let me have a think.

"It was the year we all went," I say. "Your lot, and Sandra and Dave and the kids."

"Ninety-eight?"

Back To The Future. That's the film. So bloody forgetful recently. Willow's always having a go at me for forgetting, and then she gets a rise out of calling me Grandma and so on. Which I don't mind so much because Becky is due soon. Then she can call me Grandma all she likes.

"I showed the photo to Doug," I say.

That's my husband.

She relaxes a little when she hears his name.

She asks how he is doing.

She always did have a soft spot for him.

He's a great man.

"He's great," I say.

"All clear?"

Talking about his balls.

She must have heard about that from either Shirley or Debs.

Or Facebook.

"Yup," I say. "Only got the one out of two now, but alive and well, bless him."

"That's wonderful."

"Alfie keeps calling him Hitler."

Grandma and Hitler.

What a pair.

"Why's that?" says Helen.

She's squinting through the sun.

"Because Hitler only had one ball," I tell her.

"Did he?"

I laugh.

"The other is in the Albert Hall," I say.

"I never knew that."

"You do now, Helen, you do now."

What an odd conversation all of a sudden. And here of all places. The Tip. That's what we've always called it. The Recycling Centre is its real name. The Tip, though, the Tip. The smell of the place is almost unbearable when you first drive in but you soon get used to it, and on a sunny day like this it's as bad as it will ever be. There's a loop of about twenty huge containers with crushers on top, and metal steps leading up them. We're at the end of the loop. Wood and Non-Recyclable. On the other side of the loop, we can see a man and his kid heaving a chunky television out of an Estate into TV. The kind of television that should really be extinct by now. And there's this dainty old couple emptying bags of garden clippings into Garden, taking their sweet time, as that's all they have scheduled for the day. That will be Doug and I soon enough.

You can see the Cathedral from here.

"Look," I say. "The Cathedral."

I point behind Helen.

She turns.

Her hair is pretty thin at the back now.

"Oh yeah," she says.

Forming a cap with her hand.

"Would you believe it?" I say.

"I had no idea we were so close."

I say: "so much horseshit next door to so much beauty."

I have no idea what that means.

No idea why I said it.

And why just horseshit.

The brain is a wonderful thing.

"That's life, really, isn't it?" she says.

I nod.

Thank God she understands.

She wouldn't have said something like that twelve years ago. She's going the same way as her mother, maybe. What was her name? The woman was a right depressive. Very kind towards the kids though. Kind enough. But Helen used to tell us about these moods her mother had, sometimes for days, where she just wouldn't talk. Sometimes she wouldn't even eat. Mary? No that's not it.

"What're you getting rid of today then?" I ask.

That came out wrong.

Could have phrased it better considering what's happened with Clayton.

Helen looks down.

"I mean," I say. "What's in the boot?"

"Nothing really."

"You must be chucking out something."

"Only a few things from the house."

"Right," I say.

"A little clear out."

She's being awful cagey.

What's in that boot?

A body?

Maybe she followed through and killed Clayton after she kicked him out? But, no. I joke. I saw him post some photos of animals on Paddy's

Instagram last night. So the boy is definitely alive.

"What about you?" she asks.

"Me," I say. "Oh, our old kitchen."

"You're getting a new one finally?"

"Well, the old one's over eleven years old now."

"Oh."

"Ancient."

"Quite," she says.

"We must have had that put in, you know, a while back now."

How else do you say it?

We had it fitted just after we stopped talking.

"Time for something new," she says.

I'm still trying to remember her mother's name.

Marge? Marion? Mable?

It's no good.

"How's your mum keeping?" I say.

Helen closes her lips together.

"She's not with us anymore," she says.

"Oh crumbs."

Now I definitely can't ask what her name was.

"Heart attack in the end," she says.

I say: "at least it was quick."

What else is there to say?

"That's what Phil said," she says.

Exactly.

Phil's her younger brother.

She's got two others. Maybe even three.

No husband.

"How long ago was that?" I ask.

"Four years in August," she says.

"I never knew."

Meaning: I never saw anything about this on Facebook.

How could something like that slip under the radar in this day and age?

How does anything?

"Fantastic send off," she says.

"I bet it was?"

"Even Clayton was on best behaviour that day."

"I bet he was?"

"Anyway," she says. "I should let you get on."

She turns her feet towards her car.

That scrappy old thing.

Grabs keys from back pocket.

"Actually," I say.

"Yeah?"

"Would you mind giving me a hand with the rest of this?"

Monica! Her name was Monica.

God rest her soul.

Helen used to complain and call her Monica Gone-Wrong-Ica whenever she was in one of her moods.

Imagine that.

Lovely lady.

"Of course not," says Helen.

We walk over to my Audi.

I realise it might seem like a bit of a dickhead move, as Paddy would say, to show her my car, my shiny black car, given the state of hers. But I just wanted to keep her talking. I'd almost forgotten I had an Audi. I'm being serious. I didn't have one twelve years ago. I almost forgot. The brain, you know. We barely had anything back then. I just wanted to keep her talking. Besides, there was hardly anything left in the boot. I'd already chucked most of it. Anyway, I hand her a bit of sideboard and I grab a door which used to be on the front of our dishwasher. We walk up the metal steps and throw the scraps into the Wood container. The sideboard splits in half as it lands. I tell her that it was a good shot.

I say: "Why do people let this kind of thing happen?"

"What?" she says.

"We were such good friends and now twelve years have gone by."

I spread my arms out wide and shrug my shoulders.

As if only a long-armed shrug could explain it.

"Has it really been that long?" she says.

"Almost twelve."

"You've got a good memory," she says.

"You must be joking."

"That was pretty much when it all started."

She's talking about Clayton.

"I'm sorry about what happened," she says.

She says it quickly.

Talking about the time Clayton pushed Becky down the stairs.

The same Becky that's pregnant now.

He used to do things like that all the time.

"Don't ever apologise," I say.

"Tell Sandra I'm sorry, won't you?"

"He was an evil child, Helen."

"Not evil."

No, not evil.

There is no such thing.

"Twisted?" I say.

She looks at me.

Fixes those peepers on mine.

"He was broken," she says. "He still is."

I shake my head.

"Only now," she says. "He's old enough to be broken elsewhere."

"You did the right thing, Helen."

"I couldn't kick him out before now, my own son."

"And legally a no-no."

"Exactly."

"You did the right thing."

"You should be glad it wasn't one of yours."

"I am."

"Could happen to anyone, you know. I swear by that. Anyone can end up with a bad egg. Sometimes they just go bad. No matter how hard you try, or how good your intentions are, sometimes they're just broken, you know?"

"To think Paddy and him used to be best buddies."

"And now he's terrified of him?"

"He is," I say.

"How do you think Ken and the girls felt?"

I take her hand.

I can't help myself.

"We should have helped more," I say.

We really should have.

Doug should have stepped in.

"You couldn't have done anything. Nobody could. He wasn't abusive, or anything."

"So he never hit you?"

I'd been dying to find out about that.

"Not once."

"That's good, that's a good thing."

"But he was nasty. Obsessive. Like you say – twisted."

"Such a shame."

"Let me show you this," she says.

She takes my hand and leads me down the steps to her car.

A lot of energy all of a sudden.

She unlocks it by sticking the key in the hole.

That's how old it is.

She pops open the boot and tells me to take a look inside.

I'm slightly terrified.

Maybe it's Clayton's head after all?

Shit, she's a psycho.

But no.

False alarm.

Just a bag of toys.

Or at least they look like toys. Helen delves in and grabs one of them. It's a pheasant with the head of a weasel, or a ferret, or something like that. Super realistic. But really strange.

"It's all of his animals," she says.

"What animals?"

"You know – his what are they called, taxidermies."

I take a step back.

I ask if they're real.

"They were once," says Helen.

"He killed them?"

"Some of them, some he bought on epay."

"Ebay?"

"That's the one."

I go to pick one up, arm leaning into the boot, but then withdraw my hand.

And shiver.

"I had no idea," I say.

"So I'm getting rid of them."

"Quite right."

"Daisy keeps wanting to play with them, but I just want them out of the house. I mean, look at this one."

She rummages through another bag.

She lays out a stiff creature on her outspread palm.

"Is that a rat?"

"With the wings of a kingfisher."

"My God."

We stand there for a while just staring at the rat with bright blue wings of a kingfisher.

"I'll help you get rid of them," I say.

"You will?" she says. "I didn't even know what container to put them in."

She looks up at the sign above the container.

It says Non-Recyclable.

"Non-Recyclable sounds about right."

I take two bags, and she takes two.

They're heavier than they look.

The fact that they are heavy makes me want to puke.

And the smell all of a sudden.

The same smell that's been there all along.

We climb the metal steps. She goes first. She takes it slow. One leg after the other. She complains that her legs aren't what they used to be. And I'm thankful she's going slow. Jeez, Grandma can't come soon enough. To think Clayton and Becky used to play in the sea together. We reach the platform. We peer into the black pit of everything that can't be used ever again. The stuff that doesn't get a second chance. I start to feel a little bit epic. As if this is a moment. I look at Helen, and Helen looks at me. She nods. And she tips her first bag into the container. Arms and heads and wings and tails tumble out of the bag. A rabbit thuds onto the side and then flops onto some vinyl. It has the head of something else but I can't work out what exactly. Helen smiles at me. I tell her that we should go for coffee sometime next week. Maybe we will, maybe we won't. I'll leave it in her court. I take my bag and balance it on the side of the container. I feel a bone with my finger. My God. And as I push the bag overboard a cloud of feathers erupt in a sharp, swift puff. All kinds of feathers. As if a flock of birds had exploded in front of our faces, our scared little faces. You should have seen us. Every feather you could ever imagine. In our hair. Up our noses. Floating as if set free. Feathers everywhere.

Jane Eaton Hamilton

Jane Eaton Hamilton is the Canadian author of eight books of short fiction and poetry. Her memoir *Mondays are Yellow, Sundays are Grey*, retitled *No More Hurt*, was a *Sunday Times* bestseller and included on the Guardian's Best Books of the Year list. She is the two-time winner of Canada's prestigious CBC Literary Award for fiction (2003/2014). Her work is included in *The Journey Prize Anthology, Best Canadian Short Stories* and appears in publications such as Salon, *NY Times, Seventeen magazine, MS blog, Full Grown People*. She is also a photographer and visual artist. She lives in Vancouver. janeeatonhamilton.wordpress.com.

The River of Running Sand

They come every night when the tourists go and lock us up. Every night. You can padlock a rice field, as it turns out.

You know how to lock a life?

Just take away its papers.

I hate my mother. Here is what I think when I am on my sleeping mat, and our situation hasn't changed from the day before, or the day before that, stretching back into forever, and my mother's lips pouf out with snores: I want to choke her. I calculate the fingers I'd need: 22.

(Hours to unwind her. Or metal cutters.)

She promises she'll get us out of here, to the land of milk and honey.

I say back to the hills? I've never seen the hills, but I know the winds blow jasmine and the rain drinks mango water. There is another spot, a plain, that the trees speak of, where the sands run like a river. Ancestral lands. Before this. Before Thailand. Before Burma. Before before.

She says we'll fly in an airplane. Through the Milky Way to Canada where women are the colour of bamboo sprouts.

I see Canadian women here every day; I listen to them coo over my scarves. One gave me an Air Canada pin. But they all are short-necked; they have no power here.

And my mother is a liar.

I am friends with Auwut, the Pu Yai Ban who makes big in the guard hut. Girls are rice rats giggling around him as he squares his shoulders; he has trinkets in his pressed blue shirt, western things like lipstick. But I am not one of them, I am not one of the simpering girls; I meet him later, alone, under the betel palms, where I trade for ya ba. When he leans close to me, his smile blood-red, his voice smells like krathiam.

Here's what I know, what everyone knows: Auwut has touched the ghost of a K'la, the spirits that float menace with swords and spears. Everyone insect-whispers this, worried, worried.

Auwut is a man with no soul.

But, then, so what? I am a girl without a soul. That is what my mother says.

I trade Auwut for girls smaller than me. *Eh, she is juicy like watermelon, mangosteen plump, rambut smooth.* I draw the girls in the air. A deal, a deal. *You can touch their breasts. Only their breasts, you understand?* Then, later, when everyone else is sleeping, when my mother is snoring like dingos, I sell Auwut's pink pills for a huge sum, to the doctor, out in the tobacco fields with the nicotiana. If the moon snarls behind clouds, the omen is bad. If the ducks quack in their nighttime, the omen is good.

For the smell of vanilla, an army of K'la would fall. The doctor smokes it from a tin plate on which his wife this night served him nya u.

I hoard the money for passage to Canada in plain sight. If anyone opened their eyes, they would see every bhat.

In the morning, the tourists pour in like ants down a coconut drip. Mü Kaw li, the serpent, teaches many day-to-day things about village life, but not one of these has anything to do with *here*. Here we have no village life. Here we vend. Here we make handicrafts for cash. Like most women 15 coils heavy, I weave. My back-strap loom is my very own ya ba – I weave and I am vacant with madness. I grin at tourists, pose for photographs, practice my English and sell my goods. When they ask, I pass them an information sheet which explains in German, Dutch, Spanish, French, Russian, Chinese, Japanese, Filipino, Portuguese and English that our necks are not actually elongated but instead our cervical spines and shoulders have been pushed down by the yearly addition of a new brass ring.

Yes, it is true that we leave our coils on at all times.

Yes, it's true that we cannot bend our necks.

Yes, it is true that, theoretically, our necks, weakened, could snap if we took off our coils.

Yes, it is true that we don't know the history of the custom.

Yes, it is true that the coils are brass and can weigh up to 20 pounds.

Yes, it's true that we look misshapen. Thank you for pointing this out.

Madam, would you like to try one on? Madam, would you like to purchase one to take back to Charleston, Madrid, Leningrad, Lima?

I discover that the land of milk and honey isn't Canada after all. Canada is the land of maple syrup and beavers.

I weave the patterns of seeds, cowries, python skin. I weave in diamonds, blue, green, yellow. Squares, red, black. Lines, pink, orange. My weavings limp behind me on a line. All day until we close at 5.

One tourist reaches to touch my batten. Warp, weft, heddle rod, leash cord. Thread. She runs her palm over the pattern I have woven, looks straight into my eyes. I surface out of ether. For a moment we are locked like this. "I am Lucinda."

I grunt. I won't share my name. I do not owe her my name.

She says, "Doesn't your brain rot?"

What did she just say? I only wish my English was so bad that I don't know. When we emigrate, I'll be ready. I look away, pretend I didn't understand, and eventually she leaves.

Doesn't my brain *rot*?

This is a refugee camp from five generations back. We are not free. Tourists are charged $500 bhat admission. We live fenced as zoo exhibits.

I was born in Thailand, but I am not Thai. Neither am I Burmese. I have no country. I cannot vote. I cannot rent an apartment. I cannot open a bank account. I cannot enroll in a school. I cannot drive a motorcycle. If I have a child, my child will be stateless.

In the olden days, in Burma, women like my mother, women who no longer have purpose, who have 25 coils and too elaborate a headdress, who only eat and defecate and have no husband and can hope to give nothing back, who are full of dreams but no plans, would have been driven out into the forests.

Our ancestors were wise.

"Useless old woman," I say. "If we leave it to you, we'll be here until we all die."

"Mind your tongue," she says and snaps her fingers against my arm.

"You have very miserable K'la."

Finally, I save enough to buy one set of forged papers. I count the cash when everyone else sleeps. Once I have papers, once I exist, I will be able to leave this camp and travel south to Bangkok, and after Bangkok – Canada, beavers and moose. Then, someday, a long time from now, back to the river of running sand.

I give the money to Auwut beside the chili plant when the sky is as dark as a heart, carefully explaining that this time I don't want the madness pills.

But the man is jittery as a newborn goat, smelling of mud and ya ba vanilla and something terrible, like ripping a rock away to smell a garbage pit. He grabs me and kisses me as if his kisses are what I have purchased. My lips don't move under his, I batter at him, yet his tongue comes forward like Mü Kaw li and he scoops my breasts like guavas. Another man steps forward, and then another man after him. They aren't Karen like Auwun – they are Thai Chinese with oily skin and shit odours.

"Mother," I say when her face swims into view. My K'la's ghosts huddle in the corners snapping locks shut and barking. I don't know where I am or what has happened to me or why I melt with gratitude just to see her, but at least I know that the walls are white and that I never want to let go of her, ever.

I lift my arms from the bed and wind my fingers around her neck, around her coils.

"My baby," she says, crooning a lullaby.

"My mother," I say. My fingers climb the brass, a ladder, clawing at her to keep her with me. I am broken. I can feel it where I can't feel it.

"I got papers," she says.

"Papers?"

"From the non-profit because of this. For all of us."

My K'la's ghosts grumble and recede, fading into the walls.

I look at my hands on her neck; I have betrayed her a thousand times a thousand ways. "Papers?" I ask again.

"We're going to Canada," she says. "The land of milk and honey."

Her coils gleam. My mother has done this thing, the emigration thing, succeeded where with youth and cunning I failed.

"The land of maple syrup," I say.

"Canada," she says. She takes each of my hands from her neck and kisses them in turn, then lies them along the sides of the legs I cannot feel.

Mark Illis

Mark Illis has had three novels published by Bloomsbury, and more recently two by Salt, *Tender* and *The Last Word*. His short stories have appeared in many magazines and anthologies. Mark's also had three radio plays broadcast, and has written extensively for television. He has also written the screenplay for *Before Dawn*, which won the Best Screenplay award at the Bram Stoker International Film Festival. He lives in Yorkshire with his wife and two children, and is currently writing a Young Adult novel.

Airtight

The caramel carpet was so deep and spongy, Dominic thought it might stick to the soles of his shoes. He approached the floor-to-ceiling window, pressed his fingertips against the cool glass, stared out at a sliver of St Paul's. His heart was beating against his ribs like it wanted to get out, he half expected to look down and see his lucky suit vibrating with each impact. He laid his notes at one end of the long, oval desk, checked his screen was working, took a few deep, slow breaths, and then smiled as God floated in, followed by Liam, who was His new acolyte, followed by the rest of the sycophants, flavours of the month and scared disciples.

Dominic had been writing marketing strategies before God joined the company. He'd probably been writing them before God even left university. And that didn't mean he was some old relic, some Willy Loman type who didn't understand the world had moved on. The product was a wireless, high speed, high-res, multi-compatible printer and scanner synched with all your devices. You could switch it on while you were on your way home, it was maybe one generation away from heating up your curry and recording Newsnight for you, and Dominic knew it intimately.

But he was feeling a little tense. *Relax*, he thought. *Deep, slow breaths.*

God nodded His head towards him, and said one toneless word. 'Please.'

So he began. His strategy made full use of social media, viral this and online that, upvotes and likes and retweets, while hitting the key points of *One*, positioning the product to destroy the competition, *Two*, reaching out to new customers and *Three*, encouraging upgrades by existing customers. The research was strong, the budget realistic, the focus group onside, it was all in place, and Dominic came to the end of his presentation feeling satisfied, feeling pleased with himself.

Good job, he thought, as he finished. *Nice.*

'Questions?' he said.

God gazed silently at Dominic for a long, long four seconds, then He opened His mouth and He smote Dominic's strategy with thunderbolts, He unrolled the Red Sea over it, He blasted it with seven plagues, and He did all that with relish, with an unmistakeable smirk on His smarmy, divine face.

Bastard. Callous, let-them-suffer, sadistic bastard. Dominic hoped His Son died painfully, and He ended up abandoned and lonely, bereft of worshippers, wondering where it had all gone wrong.

That's what Dominic was thinking when he was back in his office, failing to write a briefing for his team, failing to keep his temper, just generally failing. He was still thinking that way as the tube rattled and groaned towards Southgate. When his mother got cross, she used to say she was *seething*. For the first time, he understood. His rage was making him short of breath.

A young man sitting opposite caught his eye, then quickly looked away. Dominic realised he must look furious, but there was nothing he could do about it. He was having trouble controlling his face. For a while, he'd been the golden boy at work – not recently admittedly, but still, it wasn't the prehistoric era. Now, apparently, he couldn't do anything right. He was teetering, as far as he could tell, on the edge of the sack. How did that happen?

Bits of his face were actually quivering. He shielded his mouth with his hand, closed his eyes.

It wasn't his fault, it was down to his boss, He would infuriate anybody. The guy was reclining on a cloud, He had a brilliant light shining behind Him, He floated down corridors, a foot off the floor, laying down His Commandments like holiness was His natural state.

Dominic was still ranting inwardly as he walked the ten minutes from the station to his front door, and he didn't stop as he poured himself some wine, took off his jacket and tie, got dinner on. He made a double portion of bolognaise sauce and checked the cupboard for tupperware. He found an old cottage cheese pot and an ice-cream carton. Not enough. He checked the fridge, ate yesterday's salad, greasy with dressing, then washed the soup carton it had been stored in. His movements jerky, his muscles tight. Slowly, slowly, trying to get his breathing under control. He made a note and stuck it on the corkboard by the door.

MORE TUPPERWARE.

Jake came in, taking headphones out of his ears, yawning as if he'd just got up.

'How'd the thing go?'

Dominic looked at him. 'The thing?'

'The thing with the printer. How'd it go?'

Of course. Now God was going to make him look small in front of his eleven-year-old son. God was going to make him look like a failure. Jake had helped him with the PowerPoint, taken an uncharacteristic interest, told him he was going to 'smash it'.

'Yes,' Dominic said. 'Great, it was great.'

Gemma came home as he was rattling the fusilli into a pan. She was beaming.

'It's been a tears day today, full on, lake of tears. This morning, this mum, widowed, can't cope with her stepson, poor soul. I had a good, long session with her, lots of tea, copious weeping, but I pointed her towards the right agencies, got her set up with counselling, and I think I really did good, I mean I literally Did Some Good. Then this afternoon, this kid with issues, stacks of issues, trouble at school, seriously aggressive, on the spectrum, but a good heart. Guess what? By the end he was in tears too, and he let me hug him, and inside I was like Yes!'

She did a fist pump. She'd been out of work for a long time and now suddenly – it seemed sudden – she was in work again, and she adored it.

She kissed Jake, who offered the top of his head, and Dominic. 'How about you?' she said. 'You had the thingy, didn't you. The presentation?'

Dominic turned the heat down under the pasta. Seven weeks, he'd been working on it. Seven weeks.

'Yes,' he said. 'Great, it was great.'

They ate, then Dominic put the extra sauce into the three available tupperware containers, (soup, ice-cream, cottage cheese), and stashed them in the freezer.

'We need more tupperware,' he told Gemma. 'I'll get some tomorrow.'

In fact he ordered it that night. He came to bed and she was sitting up, leaning on pillows, with her laptop on her lap, tap-tapping away. It made an irritating, insect-like noise. Chik, chik, chik. He glanced at her screen, but only briefly, she got annoyed if he read over her shoulder. (She was buying shoes for Jake.) That noise could really get on his nerves if he let it, it could make his chest feel tight and uncomfortable, so he got his own laptop out, put Tupperware into his ethical search engine, and found sites offering careers in tupperware, collectible tupperware and, finally, tupperware for sale. He bought a generous amount. As he was doing so, Gemma leant over and checked his screen. There was a large graphic of a fifties style housewife filling one side of it, she had a wide Alice band in her ample hair, and she was wearing something in pale blue gingham that might possibly be called a house-dress.

'Do you wish I was like that?' she said.

He made an appreciative sound. 'Now you mention it ...'

She kissed him. 'Why are we on our laptops in bed?'

They snapped them shut.

When he held Gemma, he felt better, more sure of himself, as if someone had listened to him and agreed with what he had to say, but later, lying in the dark listening to her breathing, he was angry again, he was furious, and he couldn't sleep.

God had sent Liam to help him 'restructure his strategy'. This was tricky, since Liam was a true believer, whereas Dominic was definitely an atheist. His work was fine, it needed the odd tweak, that was all.

They quarrelled.

'You going to be like this all day?'

'Like what?'

Liam's shirt was whiter than Dominic's shirts ever were, it shone, you could probably use it to read by in a dark room. His purple tie was glossy, ecclesiastical. And he was almost a quarter of a century younger than Dominic.

'Obstructive.'

'I'm not being obstructive.'

'Yes mate, you are.'

So Dominic went to visit God. He had a corner office above the Conference Room. His spongy carpet was the colour of a robust red wine, His floor-to-ceiling windows stared out at a slightly more elevated view of the sliver of St Paul's, His desk was highly polished walnut, and He had a sofa too, and a coffee table. It was like a sitting room, except that it was nothing like a sitting room.

Dominic was planning to have a reasonable chat, to sit down and talk it out, but God was sitting on a fluffy white cloud with an infinitely-holier-than-thou expression on His face, and before Dominic had even opened his mouth He said 'I know what you're thinking,' which wasn't fair. Dominic started to speak, but God shook his head.

'I know,' He repeated.

Dominic sat on the too-low sofa. He was having trouble inhaling. 'Can I take some time off?' He hadn't expected these words to fall out of his mouth, but a break suddenly seemed like an excellent idea.

'Are you committed to the company?' God's voice wasn't deep and resonant, it was like a sharp, jabbing instrument.

Dominic was having trouble exhaling, too. His chest was like a clenched fist. He knew there was no point in lying to God. 'I enjoy my work,' he tried. He used to enjoy it, perhaps that was close enough to the truth to slip past God's omniscient gaze.

Silence. God observed him. Perhaps He'd read about the four second pause in a business manual. *How To Make Your Employees Uncomfortable.* 'Yes,' He said, finally. 'A break is a good idea. A sabbatical. Shall we say three months on half pay?'

Dominic had been thinking one month, and he hadn't considered the question of pay, but he didn't allow his expression to change. He nodded, as if this was exactly what he'd been hoping for.

'Three months,' he said. 'Thank you.'

'H.R. will facilitate,' said God.

'Of course.'

'And then,' He continued, 'we'll see.'

Dominic kept his face composed. He kept his emotions controlled. He thanked God, returned to his office, and sent an e-mail to his Deputy. *I've managed to wangle some time off* ... Printed out some notes on on-going projects, slipped them into his bag, and deleted the files. He didn't want his work being pinched. He hesitated over the photo of Gemma and Jake (grinning with crinkled eyes on a Spanish, or possibly Greek, beach), but left it there. Removing it would seem too permanent. He collected his favourite biro, the fat silver one with a bit of heft to it, that Gemma had given him.

That was it, that was all he had to do. He walked out. Face still composed, emotions still sternly controlled. A smile and a nod for Security, and he was out. He was out. He was free.

That's how he wanted to feel, he wanted to feel free, liberated, he wanted to jog down the road with an uncontrollable smile smearing his face, but he'd never been on very close terms with joy, he'd never been able to manage *insouciant*. The notion of divorcing effort from life was entirely foreign to him. So he felt concerned instead. Trepidatious. What was he going to do for three months? And *We'll see*. What exactly did that mean? He was in his mid-forties. He was actually forty-seven, he wouldn't call it late forties for another year, but anyway he definitely wasn't ready to retire. If he'd been running a hundred metre race he would be accelerating at this point, not slowing down.

His bones felt heavy and awkward, and he was still having difficulty breathing. That couldn't be good. He stopped. He stopped, as it happened, outside a kitchen supply shop.

A large parcel had been left in the bin-shed by the door. He took in his bags along with the parcel, then unwrapped last night's and today's purchases on the kitchen table. He hadn't intended to buy more tupperware, but he'd found it soothing to do so. The shop had been clean and well-lit, and full of things intended to make life easier and more pleasant.

And now the table-top was entirely covered by a blocky, featureless city. He hadn't realised tupperware came in so many sizes and shapes. Large and small, deep and shallow, curved and angular, families nesting inside each other, milkily opaque or transparent. He could box up his entire life with what lay on the table in front of him. He took out his chunky silver biro, placed it into a large square box, clicked the lid into place, then sat at the table and looked up at the recessed lights in the ceiling.

We'll see.

When Jake came home Dominic was browning the chicken, vigorously chopping an onion and some peppers.

'Hey Dad, thought you were home late, tonight?'

He shrugged, made a sound.

Jake opened a cupboard, and then gasped. 'Whoa!'

Dominic looked over his shoulder. The shelves were stuffed with plastic boxes.

'Been tidying.' He was straining to sound casual. 'Bit of sorting out.'

Jake was laughing. 'Just a bit?' He opened another cupboard, and found more plastic boxes. Dominic was reminded of that *Star Trek* episode, in which Tribbles filled every cavity on the Enterprise. It started off funny, then through some plot device that he couldn't recall, it became dangerous.

'What's going on, Dad?'

And Jake was laughing at him. Dominic could have laughed along, but he wasn't in the mood, he wasn't anywhere near that sort of mood. For the last twenty minutes he'd been getting hot clattering the heavy frying pan on the hob, his breathing had been laboured, he was pretty sure his heart rate wasn't healthy, he'd been rat-tatting the knife on the chopping board, narrowly missing his fingers, and now his son was laughing at him.

'What?' he snapped. 'Something you want to say?'

Jake took half a step back. 'I just want the peanut butter.'

'When was the last time you tidied anything up? Or pulled your weight? Or did anything useful at all?'

'Sorry.'

'Get out, go and do your homework.'

Jake went. His head was lowered and his shoulders were tight and he didn't quite dare to slam the door. Dominic watched him go, and thought of the other option, the one where he laughed along with his son, where by example he taught him insouciance, and joy.

After that, the meal wasn't very good. It was cooked, he wasn't going to poison his family, but there was something wrong with the textures and the flavour. It tasted of his temper.

Gemma's gaze darted between him and Jake.

'What's up with you two?'

No answer.

'I suggest you sort it out.'

But he didn't. He drank too much, watched TV till past midnight, came to bed when Gemma was already asleep. The next day was Saturday, and he woke late to find her sitting fully dressed on the bed beside him.

'I have the autistic kids' group,' she said. 'I told you.'

He nodded like he remembered.

'But I can stay. Will you tell me what's wrong?'

He sighed.

So she went, and after a while he got up and pulled on a dressing gown. As soon as he was on his feet, his breathing was effortful. It didn't feel as if there was a blockage, it was a deeper problem, in his chest, as if his lungs were made out of some thick, unyielding material. He stood still, waiting for it to pass, wondering what would happen if it didn't.

He was going to have a drink of water, and then he was going to find

Jake and apologise, but when he was downstairs he realised there was a bird in the house. He assumed it was a bird. It was crashing around behind the closed door of the TV room, knocking things over in a startled flurry, butting the window. It sounded like a larger animal, maybe a tiger. He tried to imagine the circumstances in which a tiger might be in the TV room, gave up. It was a bird, flying in circles, probably damaged by now. If birds could scream it would be screaming.

Maybe it was larger than he was imagining, not a tiger but a heron. There was a heron that flew over the house sometimes, that stole frogs from the tiny pond in the garden. Could a heron have got into his house, a fragile assembly of feathers and bamboo limbs clattering down the chimney?

He opened the door a crack, and looked in. A shape blurred across his vision. It was a chaffinch, about as large as his fist, with a rusty red body and a blue cap. He slipped into the room, closed the door behind him, opened the window wide and slipped out again. He waited, listening. All quiet. After a few minutes, he looked in again, and saw the bird was still there, sitting in the corner now, trembling.

There were plenty of empty tupperware boxes left over. He chose one, and went back to the TV room. The bird hadn't moved, and he wondered if it was dead. Its heart would be about the size of his fingernail. Perhaps it had simply stopped. Dominic approached the still creature slowly, cautiously, as if he was the one who was afraid, then he lifted the lid of the box, and swept it inside.

He was a man with a bird in a box. He was a man with a box full of panic. Or a box full of death. Holding it in front of his chest, he left the room and headed for the back door. He didn't want to put the box down, so he held it squashed against his body with one hand, while opening the door with the other. Keeping the box level, moving slowly, trying to transmit calmness through his dressing gown, through his ribs. The bird still wasn't moving.

Barefoot, he stepped out on to the damp grass and knelt, ready to open the box. He got his fingers under the lid.

'What you doing, Dad?'

He turned as he lifted the lid. Jake was coming out of the back door. Dominic smiled, he managed a smile, because he felt an enormous sense of relief when he saw his son. Then he turned back and found that the bird had vanished, and the tupperware box was empty except for his fat silver biro, lying there like an unexpected gift.

Ríona Judge McCormack

Ríona Judge McCormack has spent nine years working in the international development sector, and has lived and worked in Cambodia and South Africa, as well as her native Ireland. She is currently shortlisted for a 2015 Hennessey Literary Award, and has been shortlisted for both the Fish International Short Story and Flash Fiction Prizes. Her fiction and non-fiction work has been published in the *Irish Times, New Irish Writing, Sassafras Literary Magazine, Southword* and *F(r)iction Series.* She currently lives in Johannesburg, where she is completing her first novel. Twitter:@rionajmc

Stafford Street

Emily Nxumalo does not see the house for herself until the day of the auction. Her husband Walter had returned to their two-room in Orlando West one evening clutching the papers, and she had known from the paling of his knuckles that some manner of decision in her life had already been taken.

– This is it, Walter had said, his face fiercely vulnerable.

He had worked it out for her in soft pencil on the back of one of her Grade Ten copybooks. What they could gather together from family, their savings, the bank. What some of the repairs might cost. How much they could put away in the first five years, if they were careful, if they took in a student, if she went back to work after the baby was born.

– We could have your mama come to stay, he had said, and Emily had understood that he was offering her this as a proof of faith.

So she goes. She stands in the shade of a twisted tree in the front garden, the soil beneath it burnt bare, and works on emptying her face.

– Come, Walter calls from the dark rectangle of the doorway.

The agent is a softly plump woman with brittle hair. Emily watches her hands while she talks. They pull at each other, like small animals cooped up together. There are few others at the auction: a suited man, a desultory couple.

– A bargain, Walter says as they sign the deeds. – Our own house in a good area.

Which means, in this city, a white area. And she sees it in the new neighbours' faces over those first few weeks, the quick calculation of their own falling property value per black family moving in to Stafford Street.

Walter loves the stolid whiteness of that name – Stafford – nested among other old colonial imports: Thornton, Dover, Aberdeen. But then his own name, hers, are imports too.

– Our babies won't have these names, she whispers to him in the darkness of their new bedroom. – Will they?

– What names?

– You know: Walter, Emily. *Nelson.*

He shifts in the bed, warm and sleep-lazy. – Hmmm?

– Say they'll have good names. Their own names.

For a moment she thinks he has fallen back into the silence of sleep. Then he puts his mouth to her ear so that she feels his words in the small bones there: – Mafungwashe. Thanduxolo. Zimkhitha. Sibongiseni.

She laughs, low and warm, and he moves one hand over her rounded belly, tracing the curve.

– Nomathamsanqa, he says, turning her on her side, looking for access. – Vuyokazi. Kungayoimithandazi.

The tree in the front garden casts its shade into the bedroom, so that it is chill even in the dead middle of the day. She had known, from that first sighting at the auction, that the house was wrong. There is something in the way that the rooms skulk together, the spaces that do not add up. The previous people – Emily has started to think of them as *those people* – those people had painted the bedroom an ugly, violent orange, and blocked in windows with strange additions that have no use. The floors hump and fall. At the end of the passage is a tiny room with lumpen raw walls, as though the paint and plaster and concrete have been hacked back to the bones of the house.

She misses her old street – the closeness of the neighbours, the children running through doorways. The low walls and the tide of conversation. Here, she is embarrassed by the one mis-coloured door on the Fiat, its balding tires grey with road dust. She cannot invite the new neighbours in to see the broken-backed couch or the spread of mould on the ceilings. When can we fix the roof? she wants to know. In the winter, says Walter. When it is dry. When we have money.

They take in a lodger, a young man studying financial theory who leaves early and comes home late. He gives notice the second time a security patrol picks him up returning at night. She goes to the gate to shout at them.

– *Hau!* Can't you see? He is a boy with a bag of books!

The guards shift in their car seats.

– You should be ashamed!

– Ah mami, the front one says. – A mistake.

– You should be ashamed, you are black yourselves!

Walter puts a hand on her shoulder and leads her back inside. The lodger moves out that month.

When the rains come, in the sudden storms of the Highveld, water runs from the walls and pools on the linoleum. Emily can hear dripping somewhere in the ceiling, between the zinc sheeting and the boards. She hangs a piece of cloth over the hacked-out room so that it cannot look at her.

On weekends they take the highway back to Soweto and eat Sunday lunch with her family.

– When are you coming to visit? Walter asks, each time.

It is far to your place. Why we should come? Her father spreads a hand across the yard. – Everyone is here.

At school, the children gather round her belly with curious fingers. When is it coming, ma'am? they ask. Soon, she says, brushing them off. Soon. She takes the Fiat these days. Walter catches three taxis to the Clover warehouse, where he keeps his foreman's shirt in a tall locker. She is home hours earlier than he each evening, alone with the house.

She tries, at first, to scrub it out. On her hands and knees on the cigarette-pocked linoleum working to lift the grease. The house resists.

The tree, she learns, is a *Juglans nigra*. Black Walnut. Better to take it up, the man from number twenty-seven counsels. Wheeler? Wainwright? It is hard to keep track of her new neighbours' names. The man has dirt under his fingernails – no, she sees, not dirt. Earth. A rubber glove protrudes two yellow fingers from his corduroy pant-pocket; he has come from his own garden.

– Devil for the soil, he says, catching a branch and drawing it down. The leaves are long and smoothly veined.

– What an African thing to do, Walter laughs. – Take up the trees! There are no snakes here. Are you wanting that we look just like the township?

– Those trees are not good.

– It is the sign of a good house. To have trees.

She gives in then, just as she had in the face of his eager, pencilled sums. She pulls a chair out onto the cracked paving at the back of the house and settles herself there in the evenings to wait for him, her face tipped toward the sun. The leaves make a whispering above, like children at the back of a classroom. She returns inside only for tea, or when she needs to use the bathroom.

She has never slept easily, but now the baby won't let her turn. She lies on her side, watching the blooms of damp spread down from the ceiling and along the bedroom walls. Sleep comes for her in fits, spitting her back out each time. One night she becomes aware of a faint light from the living room. When she shuffles out there, bearing the weight of the child ahead of her, she sees a candle standing lit on the windowsill. It is so terrible a thing that she backs away and closes the bedroom door on it.

She could ask Walter if he had lit it. But his answer would change nothing.

From the Tswana girl living in a windowless room behind number fourteen she learns where to go. Walter does not like her speaking to the maids and the gardeners, the only people in the street to greet her properly.

– They will come calling with their hands out, he had said. – Asking: brother please. We must not start with all that.

The inyanga keeps a stall by the taxi rank in Sophiatown. He presses two fingers against her belly, *there* and *there*, humming quietly. Then he mixes bottles in the near-dark. The smoke from his fire is sweet-sour, like old meat.

– It is a crow-baby, he tells her. – It has flown in while you sleep.

Emily hides the medicine he prepares for her among the roots of the garden bushes, stoppered in an old Coca-Cola bottle. While she is digging she looks up and sees the first crow. It is waiting on the paling fence, shoulders hunched. *Kwaah*, it says.

That evening, another joins it. Emily watches them from the bedroom window, black against the black sky.

– Do you see? she asks Walter.

– See what?

Out in the darkness, the crows become four, then five.

Each afternoon, in the hours before Walter returns, she kneels at the bottom of the garden and unearths the Coca-Cola bottle. The medicine is a viscous black, gagging, awful. She retches there in the garden, kneeling beneath the whispering trees. The crows shuffle to themselves in the branches.

– *Hambani*, she tells them. – Go away.

Afterwards, the sun dances against her closed eyes. In the kitchen, the grease on the linoleum thickens; the ceiling mould blossoms in strange patterns. She finds crow-feathers in her bed.

– Who is staring? asks Walter.

The curtains are closed now, against the light. The Fiat rests on blocks in the driveway.

– Everyone, Emily says. – I see them at the windows. They do not want us here.

The baby comes on a Tuesday morning. She calls Walter from the bedroom floor, her fingers slipping on the cellphone buttons. Just as the call connects a contraction pushes all her breath out.

– Walter, she says, a pulling in of air.

She stumbles out into the back garden. On her knees, hands braced, she finds her balance. While Walter catches two taxis in reverse and sprints the distance from the drop-off, Emily breathes against the contractions, counting. Crows line the fencing. Behind her, the house watches.

Walter finds her there on the packed dirt. Her face is shining, crooning over the bundled cloth held damply against her chest. There is blood on the ground, on the leaves.

– They put a bad seed in me, Emily says, smiling. – But I took care of it.

She touches the feathers gently, cradled in the wrapping of her skirt. Around them, the houses of Stafford Street sit empty in the midday quiet, their windows blank. The crows have gone.

Paul McMichael

Paul McMichael lives in London with Marc, his partner of 28 years. He is the winner of the 2013 Bristol Short Story Prize and is delighted to be in this year's anthology. His story, *After the Rhododendrons*, was broadcast in 2013 on Irish national radio. Paul has had several stories shortlisted in various competitions including the inaugural Brighton Prize last year.

The Ice Ages

Samuel parked his bike at the back of the Centre's wooden main house. He went inside. He said hello to the manager and pushed the swing door into the kitchen and put on an apron and got stuck in to preparations for breakfast with the other volunteers. Soon the refectory doors swung open and the current residents lurched into the room. He glanced out through the serving hatch.

They were his age, sixteen or maybe seventeen, wore their hair to their shoulders, lank and unwashed, short denim jackets, inked with biro, rock bands and republican slogans – Status Quo, The Who, Brits Out, Up The Provos. They swaggered. Glared.

It was his father who had volunteered his services at the Centre for Community Reconciliation, although the Reverend William McIlrath had no fondness for what went on there. 'Ecumenical tokenism', he'd said with a sneer, 'bringing down Republican thugs and layabouts from the ghettos of West Belfast'. For Samuel it was a chance to escape stifling pieties and the prickling sensation of always being under a moral microscope, but so far his contribution to improving community relations had amounted to 'how would you like that egg?'

He moved back and forth along the row of hot pans and served food until the line thinned. Last was a tall, heavy-shouldered boy. Samuel took in the face, the battered line of the nose that wavered on the way down to the boy's chalky, bitten lips, eyes darting around. 'What'll you have?' he said to the boy, trying to sound cheerful and welcoming. 'We're out of bacon but we've plenty of sausages. And I can do more eggs?' He tried a thin smile.

'No bacon? For fuck's sake.'

Samuel's cheeks reddened.

The boy leaned in to the counter and spread himself out on both hands. 'Are them Catholic eggs?' he said.

Yes and no were a double jeopardy. Maybe it was because this was Samuel's last day, or maybe it was because this group would soon get on a coach for the journey back to the narrow streets of their own neighbourhood, but he replied, 'the brown ones are Protestant and the white ones are Catholic. But they're all nice eggs.'

The boy looked around but his friends had their heads down into their plates, wiping runny yolks with wheaten bread and shoving food eagerly down into their throats in some mad race to clear plates. He turned back to Samuel and jabbed a finger, 'toast, sausages, fried bread...and a dose of them beans.'

Samuel filled a hot plate then spooned from the tray of baked beans. Was that a dose? He dished out another tablespoonful to be sure. He spooned a third when the second got no response. The sausages swam in beans. He looked up.

'Did I say stop?' said the boy.

Samuel tipped the vessel up, scraping the sticky residue from the edges. The plate was a puddle, overflowing onto the tray. 'That's the last of the beans.'

'Aye, I see that. Do I look stupid?' The boy lifted his tray and lingered for a moment, as if there was something else he was going to say. Then he snapped his mouth shut and grabbed the tray and headed for a table.

Samuel stole a glance. The youth wore jeans with turn-ups showing the top of Doc Martens laced up past the ankle. The denim was skin tight. He couldn't help staring. A power worked within him. 'Behold my affliction, I beseech thee, for the enemy hath magnified himself'.

Imagine if these hard lads could see what was inside him, what a beating he'd get, not just for being 'a Prod'. But he couldn't help himself.

The youth turned at the table and glanced back.

Caught! Samuel jerked around and shrunk back into the kitchen, flushing with fear and anger and guilt. He cleaned up in a hurry. He didn't glance through the hatch. The room emptied and he helped clean and tidy up, get the kitchen ready for the lunch service. He went to the manager's office with the other volunteers and half listened as everyone said their goodbyes, promising to see each other next Saturday night in such and such a pub in town. Samuel just wanted to get on his bike and get away.

Outside, the sun flung itself against the bleached white boards of the building. He squinted and stumbled towards the bike and yanked it backwards into the open. He pushed and began to mount with one foot, but instead of the fast getaway from a standing start, the pedal suddenly lurched downwards, metal grinding against metal behind him. He bent down in a fluster. The chain was jammed in the rear gear wheels. It would need the proper tools to put things right. He'd have to walk it home. Still, it was mostly downhill and he'd be just about make it home for his mother's roast lamb, even if they had to put a plate over it and keep it warm.

At the edge of the car park he glanced backwards to the Centre. Denim boy was just yards behind, walking his way.

'Do you want a hand with that?' the boy said. He must have been watching the whole time.

'It needs tools,' said Samuel.

The boy's jaws worked tirelessly on pink bubble gum.

'I need to get home now,' said Samuel and tried to turn and walk away.

'Sure I'll walk with you.'

'You're alright.'

Foot steps right behind him.

'Your bus'll be leaving soon,' he said.

'It's not for ages. They'll not leave without me.' The boy popped the gum, like a full stop.

Samuel sped up. The boy followed, a little way behind. They reached the first corner. The boy was alongside now, but said nothing. Bubblegum pops. Further on, the hedgerows closed in on either side, branches of gorse curving chaotically into the road, weighed down with dense yellow flowers. Samuel could have stuck out two arms and brushed fingertips along the delicate petals on either side.

The boy sniffed the air and screwed up his nose. 'Ripe. Jeez, what's that stink?' 'It's the gorse,' said Samuel. The boy sniffed the air again. 'Cat's piss.'

Cat's piss on top but honey below, Samuel said to himself. 'Round here they call it whin.'

The boy reached a hand to a broad heavy clump of the flowers.

'No!' said Samuel. He dropped the bike and leapt to push an arm away but it was too late.

The boy snapped his hand back. 'Fuck!'

'You can't take a hold,' said Samuel.

The boy looked down at his hand. Thorny spines emerged from the fleshy parts of his fingers and around the base of his thumb. He drew in a long breath through his teeth. 'You can pull them out,' said Samuel.

The boy held out the hand for inspection. 'Are they poison?'

'No,' said Samuel. 'Here.' He took the hand in his. Pinching thumb and forefinger, he pulled at one of the thorny spines, releasing a tiny red bubble of blood.

The boy yelped and then elbowed Samuel away. 'I can do it myself,' he said. He pulled at the other needles one by one and then shook his hand and clenched his fingers, testing the aftermath. 'I'll never shoot straight again.' He looked over at Samuel.

Samuel's eyes widened.

'A joke,' said the boy. 'A joke, right? I've never held a gun. What? You think they give them out on our first day at school?'

'No,' said Samuel. 'But what do I know? You could be anyone.' He turned and made for the bike.

The boy followed, putting himself between Samuel and the bike. 'Pay no heed to my bollix,' he said. 'The name's Dermot.'

Samuel weighed up the sharing of names. It would be a delicate thing at any time. 'Samuel.'

'Sammie is it? Away on!'

'No...just Samuel.'

'Right. Samuel it is then.' He put out a hand. 'Dermot O'Neill.'

Samuel looked at the big hand. He took hold. 'Samuel McIlrath.' He let go and looked down. Spots of blood transferred to his own palm.

'Aye. Sorry about that,' said Dermot. 'It won't kill ye.'

Samuel rubbed at the drying blood and took in the hopeful look on Dermot's face. 'And neither will those Protestant eggs,' he said.

Dermot laughed. 'Aye, but the beans might,' he said, wafting away smells from under his nose.

'I thought you'd never stop,' said Samuel, 'you're half man, half bean.'

'Aye. Don't light a ciggie for a hundred yards.'

'You'll be cordoned off.'

'Like an incendiary device...' Dermot glanced at Samuel, clamped his mouth.

'We've had them here,' said Samuel after a moment then wheeled the bike around to face home. He could hear Dermot behind him, keeping a distance. The road was no more than a track now, a bit of grass and a few daring daisies sprouting up along the middle. At the brow, Samuel stopped, pointing to the right. 'See that?' he said. 'Lough Carrick.' He nodded towards the small lake trapped between low heather-covered hills and the ridge on which they stood. In the middle was an island, with a few wind-blown blackthorns clinging to a group of grey stones. 'It's man-made,' he said. He turned to Dermot. 'They've found bones. Human bones.' He watched Dermot's reaction. 'Pagan sacrifice they reckon.'

'Bollix. Are ye having me on?' said Dermot.

'Skulls cracked open, axe heads inside.' Samuel looked at Dermot's eager face, raised his game. 'Beating hearts ripped from living bodies.'

'Come on,' said Dermot with a slap to Samuel's arm. He mounted the shaky barbed wire fence and leapt over. He gestured Samuel forward. 'Come on!'

Not what Samuel had planned. 'It's Sunday. We're having lamb. My father –' 'Never you mind about your aul' Da. Will it kill him if you miss the lamb?'

'No, but –

'But nothing. Come on over and show me this wee lake.' He forced down the topmost strand of rusted barbed wire. 'Dump the bike over,' he said. 'I'll make sure you're back later for your Da.'

'Just to the lake and back, right?'

'Aye, to the lake. No bother. Come on, before this thing kills me.'

Samuel lifted the bike over then a leg. He was facing Dermot, astride the barbed wire for a second. He reached out to steady himself on Dermot's shoulder, sensing the muscles trembling with the effort to keep the fence at bay. He let go his hand and stepped all the way over.

He laughed. Relief. Dermot laughed with him. That set Samuel off and then somehow they were roaring and making a mad charge down the field. The sheep dotting the slope lifted their heads, groggily eyeing the onslaught then scattering wildly.

The terrain grew boggy and they picked their way through patches of dark reeds and outcrops of grey stone. By the water they perched on two boulders, weathered smooth and mottled with ancient lichen, looking over at the island.

Dermot searched for small stones, hefting each one for weight, then cast them far out into the lake.

Samuel watched them soar up and outward, out to where the sound of their entry into the water was muffled by the breeze.

Dermot sat down again, closer to the edge.

Samuel stared at the long hair flicking the pale skin at the back of Dermot's neck. 'That's your good throwing arm,' he said. It just came out. He meant nothing by it.

Dermot turned. A clouded face. 'Do you want me to answer that?'

Samuel had watched the news with his parents every night, a stream of dreadful news from Northern Ireland's burning cities; explosions, shootings, angry mobs facing off to the British Army between rows of burnt out terraced houses. 'Maybe I do. We're not completely stupid up here,' he said.

Dermot softened again. 'Aye,' he said, 'maybe.' He studied a pebble in his hand, then turned to Samuel. 'If I could get out, leave all that shite, you know? But you get caught up Samuel, you want to do the right thing, protect your community. Look, there's armoured cars down our street every night!' He pulled his legs up and rested a head on his knees. 'Are stones so bad?'

Samuel looked at the fine hair brushing the back of Dermot's neck, imagined him on a street corner, taut with anger. He saw himself putting out a hand, lifting Dermot's and pressing it against his own, tracing out the hard ridges on Dermot's palm, blistered from flinging fragments of the city's grey paving at men in uniform who had come to defend people like Samuel.

Dermot stood up. 'Is there a boat?'

'I...I don't think there's any fish so –

'Is there anything else on the island?'

'Not really, just those few trees. Rocks.'

Dermot swivelled left and right. 'Shite.'

Time slowed. Vague sun dappled the dark water. Samuel was going be late in any case. His father would rage at him. He'd be kept in the house. 'Stay there,' he said, 'I'll show you something you won't see in Belfast.' He got up and went a bit of the way around the lake. He took off his shoes, rolled up his trousers a good six inches. He stepped down to the edge of the water. A glance back, to make sure he was still being seen. He slowly raised his left foot and placed it onto the bog-dark surface. Then the other. He stood up straight. The lake bore him up. He took another step, then another, arms wavering in mid-air.

Dermot was off the ground, closing the gap between them, his voice loud and clear across the silent water, 'Jesus! Teenage fuckin' Jesus!'

Samuel didn't look up. He put one foot in front of the other and went forward, moving steadily, edging to the left and then right, reaching out with toes to test the next step. He reached the island and turned, waving his arms in a wide arc. He put his hands to his mouth. 'Come on! Your turn!'

Dermot was at the same spot. He looked down at the black water and shouted over. 'Away on, this is bollix, Samuel McIlrath!'

'You can do it!'

'Here? Should I walk here?'

'Go on. Right there!'

Dermot was barefoot. He put out a leg. The foot broke the surface and he pulled back. 'Cold!' He tried again. He put out the other foot. He stood up. He was standing on the lake. He roared and whooped, 'Hey! I'm Jesus!' Then he wobbled, flailing his arms to regain control.

'Careful!' Samuel shouted. 'Short steps!'

Dermot went out onto the water, steadily following Samuel's commands from the island to go left or a little to the right, until they were close.

'You need to jump now,' said Samuel.

'Jump? Did you?' Dermot was taller but heavier than Samuel.

'It's only a foot or so deep if you can't.'

'Bollix, I'll do it. I can do it.' He dipped down, lurched, then stopped and stood upright. 'I can do this.'

'Dermot, here. I'll grab you.'

'Aye?'

'Aye. Come on.'

Dermot bent low and swung his arms back and forth, shuffled from foot to foot. Then he sprang forward, with one leg outstretched, arms out high in front.

Samuel got hold of a jacket and then an arm. He pulled hard. They bowled over into a heap on the ground, Dermot's body pressed against him.

Two other boys would have laughed and moved apart.

'Wee buns. Easy,' said Dermot, still catching his breath. He looked right at Samuel then he dipped his head, his mouth meeting Samuel's, chalky bitten lips making delicate, fleeting contact.

Samuel's eyes closing, insides untethering.

Dermot rolling away and standing up in a single, loose-limbed movement, striding to the edge of the island, glancing back, a face that said 'kill me now'.

Samuel shivered. Fear. Hope.

Silence pooled at their feet.

'That could have been where they did it. Ripped out the hearts. Like an altar.' Dermot nodded towards the blackthorns where a flattish grey stone, patched with pale yellow and green lichen, stuck out. He went over to stand with an elbow against a dark trunk, treading carefully in his bare feet. 'Do you think they were cannibals?'

'Sorry?' said Samuel. He was still thinking about the kiss. Dermot switched so easily, pretending nothing had happened.

'Them that slaughtered their enemies,' said Dermot. 'A pile of bones down there?' He wiggled his toes in the scruffy grass.

'I think it was all dug over already,' said Samuel, 'there'll be no trace left now.' He shivered again and touched the place where their lips had met.

Dermot went back to the edge of the water. He skimmed stones, setting off small ripples that moved out against the lake's own low waves. 'What now? How do we get back?' he said.

'The same way. We'll have to wade to the first stone.'

'No way can I roll these up.' The denim was sodden, swollen. 'Shite. And the bus'll've cleared off without me. For fuck's sake.'

The old Dermot.

'Sure you can walk on water now,' said Samuel. 'And I'll not get home for the roast lamb.'

'Christ....' Dermot changed gear. 'Aye, your poor Ma and Da. They'll have to eat up all that lamb themselves.'

Samuel pushed himself upright. 'Time to go.'

'Aye,' said Dermot. He bent down to wrestle with his jeans. They waded the first few yards then made a halting return across the submerged causeway, then stepped through the bog, striding the upper field, not talking much. Samuel climbed the last fence himself and hauled the bike over. They were back on the narrow road. They stood there, not catching each other's eyes. After a time, Dermot broke the silence.

'I better go back up to the Centre. See about getting another bus, or staying the night,' he said.

'It was great, the lake and everything.'

'Teenage Jesus.'

'Aye. The Miracle of Lough Carrick. They'll have a shrine up.' 'Women on their knees.'

'A stall selling holy water.'

'There'll be revelations. Speaking in tongues.'

'Aye, prophesies, nuns, a thousand kinds of bollix. It does my head in sometimes.' Dermot stopped smiling. 'Well, I'd better go.' His limbs were on the move, fitful. He came over to where Samuel was standing. 'You're not bad,' he said, 'for a Prod.' He bumped a fist on Samuel's shoulder.

'And yourself, Dermot,' said Samuel. 'For a Taig.'

They both laughed.

'I'll head on,' said Dermot. He jammed two hands deep into the front pockets of his jeans and started to walk away. He got five yards then spun around. 'Shake hands?'

An insignificant thing, a handshake, thought Samuel. But this one meant yes somehow. So what was the question? Now would be the time to find out, if his jaw hadn't turned to stone, or if the jumble of words in his head dared form themselves into something like truth. Up close, Dermot's blue eyes were flecked with tiny green shards.

Those eyes would do. If he had nothing else, just those eyes would do.

The tiniest pull of coarse skin against his own palm told him it was over. Their hands untwined.

'Be seeing you around, Samuel McIlrath.' Dermot's mouth clamped shut in a grim smile. He strode up to the brow of the hill then glanced around and waved.

Samuel raised a hand but Dermot had already turned back. He kept watching until the semblance of Dermot's head blurred with the hedgerows. He waited a while longer, squinting into the distance. Then he swung the bike around and set off towards home. The bicycle took up a broken tune, chain rattling against spokes, a taunt to the turmoil inside him. He gave it a swift kick to silence the clatter.

The bogland gave way to a lusher green lower down. Somewhere in a field a tractor murmured. The bark of a dog echoed against a farmyard wall. A blackbird flew up from a stand of tall trees and arced across the wash of pale blue sky, then disappeared.

His mind circled. The wheels of the bicycle inched round. He leant the bike by a gate and sat on the grassy verge, beyond caring now if his trousers stained. He picked at the short grass, wished the day over, that he might slip home in the dark and go up to his room to ponder everything that had happened without having to see or speak to his parents. He lay back and stared at the sky, made the clouds into faces and far away cities.

He'd been kissed. He'd wanted more. The thought and the act, it was all sin, a closed circle, like the clean, thin wire of a rabbit trap, waiting to pull taut. Catholics had their confession, a Popish conceit his father had said, a get-out-of-jail-free card, forgiveness in a box. How would confession go with Dermot now, he wondered – I spat on the floor, I took the Lord's name in vain a million times, I kissed a boy on a lake island of old bones? Would the priest whisper in reply – was he a wee Prod, did he slip in a lustful pink tongue to lap at the purity of our Catholic youth?

He grabbed the bike and hurried on down to the junction with the main road.

To the left was home. His parents would be frantic by now but still he couldn't go. He turned right, down to the town. He paced the dull high street, shops shut up tight against the risk of firebombs. Who knew if an incendiary device hadn't been slipped into a pocket of a jacket at the drapers, or dropped into a bucket at the back of the hardware store, ready to ignite and engulf the shop and everything in it?

He moved on. The children's playground was deserted. He sat on a swing. He switched to the roundabout and pushed himself round until he had to get off and lie down to steady his head.

The remains of the sun mustered a purple glow that drew hungry midges from the bogs and drove him seaward. At one end of the bay was a volcanic dyke, jutting a hundred yards out into the sea. He left the bike in the dunes and crossed the wooden bridge that spanned a break in the rocks and made his way to the farthest point, where the waves foamed. He looked up at the dark curve of Knocklayde. 'The mountains shall be lowered for the coming of the Lord'.

Well, ancient ice had come and gone and scoured these mountains low and the Lord was ten thousand years too late. Or maybe He'd been already and hadn't liked what He saw up at the lake isle at Carrick, the pile of smashed bones, the way men were so easily set against one another?

He sat down and waited for the sunset. Dermot would be on a bus now, chewing gum he imagined, popping reckless bubbles to unnerve the soldiers, boys only a bit older than him, from Yorkshire and Essex, or Glasgow, at some dreary breeze-block checkpoint on the outskirts of Belfast, a last glimpse of the world outside before the divided city swallowed him up.

The sky in the west turned, a stain of pink and gold on the horizon. In

Samuel's head, Dermot's voice, as clear as if he was perched on the jagged rocks beside him; Bollix, Samuel McIlrath, complete bollix! Dermot kissing him again and then laughing, coarse fingers entwined with his, until the marine light blackened.

Fiona Mitchell

Fiona Mitchell is a features and fiction writer. This year, she won the Frome Festival Short Story Competition and her work has been shortlisted in various other competitions including the Writers' & Artists' Short Story Competition. This is the second year in a row that Fiona's work has been included in the *Bristol Short Story Prize Anthology*. Her short stories have also been published in the *Bath Short Story Award Anthology* and the *Yeovil Prize Anthology*. She has just finished a rewrite of her first novel *The Maid's Room* and is editing her second novel, while working on ideas for a third. To find out more about Fiona's work, visit https://fionamomitchell.wordpress.com and connect with her on Twitter @FionaMoMitchell

Black Lines

The coyote slogs its way towards me, stepping into the people spaces. I curl myself smaller and fix it with a snake eye. It stops in front of me, teeth bared, chest scratched with black lines.

A faraway Jay pokes the air with a *weep-weep-weep*. I try to breathe away my colour and merge with the metal grille that I'm lying on. The metal grille that every so often tries to buck me off onto the tracks below. Apart from my nose dripping, I am lizard still.

The coyote opens its jaw and hack laughs, then sinks its teeth into Mamá's shoulder. The bite sounds like the pull of a cooked chicken leg. Mamá closes her eyes and her mouth goes wavy like it does when she makes her worst kind of hurt. The coyote swaggers away, leaving teeth marks on Mamá.

I open my eyes wide and cry, 'Uh, uh, uh.'

The fat sucks from Mamá's cheeks. She slaps my face.

'Ay!' I shout.

The hand comes for me again: the picked-off *Peach Melba* on the forefinger, the *Ignite the Night* silver glittering on her thumb. Mamá's hand has been real naughty lately. Pinching me when I'm asleep. Smacking flat across my mouth. Pushing the screams down my throat. My belly is swollen with them. My ear tickles with her breath.

'I'll hit you again if you keep crying,' she says.

I swallow my tears like burps and open my book:

Snakes are covered in scales which allow them to move over hot surfaces like rocks and sand.

I run my finger along the thin, red tongue. This one doesn't look as angry as the ones chalked on the barrios walls.

The Beast leans and moans underneath me. It is hard and burn hot. It smells bad too. Like when Papi used to kiss Mamá and smoke blew from their pressed-together lips. The tops of my ears are cooked. Mamá won't let me take my trainers off. Or the black T-shirt that sticks to the badness on my back.

The land out there is dusty like her face. There are grey rocks and dry paths that curve in different directions. If I squeeze my eyes just so, it looks a pale kind of ill.

'I'm too hot,' I say.

Mamá's shoulders fill with air.

'At least you haven't got no hair to make you hotter,' she says.

She combs her hand over my shaved head. I wipe away my sweat necklace. A cottontail cracks over dry sticks. There are muskrats out there too. Fluffy animals that make me feel clever – a brown vine snake slipping through cracks. A boy spits over the side, his head low and watching.

'Look,' he says.

He's pointing, but all I see is the beige and the brown.

'Armadillo,' he says. 'He builds a shell around himself.'

The boy turns onto his back and stares at the sky. I carry on looking into the scrub. Smiles race by. Kids waving their hands at us. I wave back, then switch my eyes to Mamá who doesn't like me speaking to anyone apart from her.

When the sun is almost gone, shadows rise and fall in the parch. The

Beast is tired now and I swallow. Because bad things happen when the Beast goes slow and the light starts to fade. The shadows attach themselves to the Beast who, trying to shake them off, picks up speed again. They fall and roll away. The disappearing light shines the boy's snot like a jellyfish. Something slouches its way along the metal. Its legs and arms are loose, its eyes chasing an invisible fly. My blood rushes like the Chamelecón, but I don't cry like before. I'm a fast learner.

'Eh,' the coyote, a different one, says.

My eyes are almost closed.

'I'm talking to you,' he says, nudging Mamá with his too-long toenail. 'Double fare.'

Mamá opens her eyes.

'I don't got nothing,' she says, with a shiver of earrings.

'No fare, no ride,' he says.

'I give you money at the other side. My sister, she has money.'

'I'm not going that far,' the coyote says.

He tips onto his knees. He puts his arms around Mamá and whispers into her ear. There is a fat stick in the back of the coyote's trousers. As he jerks and sways Mamá, and Mamá makes sounds like she's swam underwater and come up for air, I put my hand on the stick. It is warm and plastic and black like my trousers. It is loose and easy to pull away. The curve at the end of it glitters. People's cheeks flicker with the light of it, their chests going fast up and down.

Mamá puffs like when she touched her hands to my bruises. There had been six of them kicking me on the ground. Their feet had thudded and purpled me. My back, my stomach, my face. I push the stick down the side of my jeans. It is a nice kind of cool on my skin.

The coyote gets up then and moves away from Mamá. His face is like paper on fire. He bends and pulls my trainers off. I stop pretending to be

155

asleep. Mamá carries on breathing loudly. Her eyes are wild and too bright. There is a warning between her close together teeth. The coyote ties the laces of my shoes together and strings them around its neck. He staggers away.

'Nah, nah, nah,' Mamá goes through her nose. The rev of a bike.

'You'll get hit if you cry,' I say in a quiet voice.

She wipes her soggy face and lays a hand on her stomach. Full with the sucked-in tears and the sounds, it is hard and round like mine.

I look at my book again: *Snakes don't have legs. They use their muscles and scales to do the walking.*

'Go to sleep,' Mamá says.

There are skeleton shadows in her face. I close my eyes so I don't have to see them.

Soon, something shakes me awake. The air around me is yellow.

'Come,' says Mamá.

She takes both our bags and swings down from the Beast.

'Come,' she hisses again.

'I can't,' I say.

'Snakes slither down trees all the time,' she says.

I get up, swallow the sticky stuff in my mouth. Mamá puts a foot on a shelf at the side of the Beast, her arm around me. There are bushes ahead. They stroke us and Mamá pulls me back and we fall.

'Ay!' I shout.

Then our legs are pedalling the air, the branches scratching us. The Beast screams away, its body sprayed with letters and lines. The branches have painted Mamá's face red. She takes my wrist and pulls me along. I snap away then slot my fingers through hers. It is a rough kind of carpet, this grass, with empty cans and plastic bags. One of the cans has Red Bull written across it. I spot three long injection things. Stones dig at my feet, but it's my back that won't let me be: all hurt and hot.

'Five!' I say.

Mamá says, 'What?'

'I've seen five of those plastic things,' I point behind me.

'Syringes,' she says. 'They're to stop sleep.'

'How?'

'There's special medicine inside them so you can stay awake for longer.'

I used to like staying up late.

Papi made me stay up late when he put the man into the ground. He dropped mud into the screaming hole with a spade. I stood with the men, my legs against the piled up rubbish, eating the air and the sounds. I said nothing; it was like my mouth was full of mud.

We come to a stream. Mamá drops the bags onto the ground, bends and licks at the water. I kneel and press my face into the trickle. It is warm, but cooler than the air. It tastes of clay. I sit in the water and my trousers suck it so fast it's like they're thirsty too. My back burns in the wet. Mamá pulls up my T-shirt and makes a sound like air squashed from a ball.

'Puto!' she says and bangs a fist to her chest.

She fills a bottle with stream water and hangs our bags from her arms. She crouches like a runner about to start a race. I curl myself to her back. She walks. Together we are a fat black shadow.

Soon, she puts me down. She takes off her trainers and ties them to my feet. I walk behind her, but there are bubbles on my heels. I take the trainers off, tie the laces together and hang them around my neck like the coyote did.

'Snakes don't need shoes,' I say.

Mamá takes a long time to undo the tight knot.

We sit and drink from the bottle that Mamá filled up at the stream. She takes a rambutan from her bag and squashes it apart. I fill my cheeks with it. She presses my head onto my bag. And when I wake up, her hair hangs around my face like a screen. She spits into her hand and rubs my cheeks with it. She gets up and pulls me behind her, hooking my elbow through hers and covering my hand. We walk for a long time. It's like knives are slicing my feet. Except I have no feet because I am a snake. I don't have feet, but I have me a knife. The steel slips against my wet skin.

The grass disappears and we are on black stuff. It is flat and hot, without stones. A truck bumps its ways towards us. There is a sign on it with numbers and letters. I've never seen a truck with one of those before. Mamá waves her hand out. The windows are see-through. I tilt my head to look at the man inside. He winds the glass down.

'We're headed north,' Mamá says. It's like there's grit in her throat.

'Oh yeah,' the man says.

Mamá's hand hurts mine as she squeezes. She breathes long and slow and noisy.

'Hop in,' the man says.

The door pops open. Mamá sits in the middle with her bag on her knee, her thigh sandwiched against the man's hairy, bare skin.

'Water there at your feet,' he says.

There is a copper band on his finger like Mamá used to wear before she screamed at Papi: 'Isn't it enough that they've taken Chilango? And now they want Milton too?'

Papi's face stayed still, his face with its three-pointed star right here on the cheek and the lines like black lace.

I look at the man driving the truck and touch the knife in my side. There are no black lines on this man's face, only a limp rag of skin under his chin. I drink the water.

'What's your name, kid?' he asks.

'Mmm,' I start.

'Marco,' says Mamá.

The man puts a box into Mamá's lap. Orange Gamesha cookies. We crunch our way through the bumps. My stomach tries to start a conversation with me.

Mamá's eyes are sleep lazy. I close mine, then open them again, my head spinning on my neck. I eat another biscuit and watch the man's hands on the wheel and Mamá, her head falling against his shoulder. I open the book and try to find my page.

Dull coloured snakes use their colouration as camouflage. And, some snakes mimic the colour and pattern of venomous snakes.

After a long time, the man turns the car sharply. Leaves and branches scrape the glass. He pulls a lever with a creak that wakes Mamá. It's only when the man turns my way that I see the scar, lined like a fat worm on his cheek. He leans far across Mamá, so far that I smell the garlic on his breath. I put my fingers around the knife. The man pulls the door handle on my side and the warm air spills in.

'There's barb all the way, but I know people who've made it across,' he says.

Mamá's eyes go the size and colour of mangosteens. I touch the corner of my book through the bag and get out. Mamá climbs out too. The truck reverses with no lights on and rumbles away.

There is a fence in front of us. It rips the blue black sky into prison bars. It is monster tall, a tangle of wire at the top like the curls I used to have before Papi shaved them off. I don't want to touch the fence, but worse things have put their arms around me. Like Chilango's, pushing me down. And the other arms, including Papi's, pushing the needle into my spine. Mamá tries to throw my bag over the fence. It misses and falls into the dirt. She tries again and still doesn't manage it.

I bite my teeth together, put the bag onto my back and climb up into the quiet of the sky, away from the insect hum. The wind slaps my face up there. My foot slips and see-saws me and the fence bites into my hand. I scramble until my foot finds another diamond-shaped hole. There is something else whirring out there. A mosquito. Loud, then louder still.

'Go quick,' Mamá hisses.

The barb hurts my hand, but I am a snake and snakes like rough crossings. I squeeze the barb down like a cushion. There is a rip of skin. The whirring is on top of us now. A flashing red bead in the sky. I push over one leg and it gets caught. I shake myself and the fence rattles. I shake so hard that Mamá shakes too.

Then I am over the top. I go down quick until Mamá's hands are touching mine through the fence. She stares at me from the other side – the eyebrows like thin pencil lines, the eyes a shock of coffee.

'Go, my boy,' she says.

'But Mamá.'

'There's no need to be a snake anymore.'

The swallowed down tears and the big sounds push their way up my throat. Hair falls into Mamá's face. She pushes it behind her ear, sniffs and raises her chin.

'You want me to come over there and clip you?' she says.

I run into the bushes. Tyres crunch gravel and Mamá is lit up, blue arms grabbing at her. She tries to sit down in mid-air, but they pull her away, yanking up her T-shirt as they go. Pushed down inside her trousers is the black handle of the knife that I found. And watching over it, on the skin of her back, is a python ready to pounce. Mamá's T-shirt falls then and covers the picture like a curtain. The darkness eats Mamá up and the car roars away, lighting up a flicker of moths.

The place is cricket loud. I add my own sound to it.

'Huh, huh, huh,' I go and the tears roll down my face because Mamá isn't there to hit me anymore.

I cry the way I did when the hand with the numbers on it came for us. It clicked the gun and pointed it at Mamá's counter covered with nail varnish bottles. The bangs hurt my ears. So did Mamá's screaming. The counter was all holes. Finger painting blobs of blues and reds and oranges, pinks and greens. A thousand pieces of glass twinkling in them.

I try to pretend that the pain in my feet isn't there. I kick the empty tin cans. I walk and I count. I walk for a long time, down steep hills, brushing against the trees, putting my hand on bark as I go. The leaves that I pass turn from yellow to green.

Much later, the trees ripple and out steps a man with a fat stomach and a walkie talkie in his hand.

'Come with me, son,' he says.

I try to lick away the snot before he sees it. I tip my chin and follow him through the green. There is a van out there on the road with a sign on the back that says Patrol. The man slides open the back door and I climb in.

'What's your name?' the man asks.

'Mmmm,' I say, then set my face like Mamá did in the truck on the other side of the fence. 'Marco.'

'Well, Marco, I'm taking you to a detention centre.' His voice is the gloop of treacle.

He passes back a bottle of water. I twist off the top and put small sips into my empty stomach. I think of Mamá in the car slicing through the night. I'm about to ask whether they will bring Mamá to where we're going, but I swallow the thought. I close my fist so I can hold onto the whisper of her fingers through the fence.

The van stops. Outside, I bite my teeth together hard when the man puts his hand on my back. The building has orange bricks and a flag dancing outside. I follow the man through spinning sheets of glass. I touch my hand to the glass; a hazy mark appears on it and the door stops spinning. The man puts his hand to my back again and I squeeze my fist harder.

Inside, the man fills out a form, then points to an arch.

'Go on now,' he says and I walk through.

Another man, this one in green overalls, touches me all over. Then a door opens to a bright white room with blankets, some of them silver. Instead of snake scales, my arms are covered in bumps and sticky-up hairs.

A woman carrying a young boy, wrapped in a yellow blanket, turns to look at me. Two men are lying down clicking cards to the floor. There are kids on a bench, arms folded, knees pulled to chests. I rub my arms and try to put some warmth into them. A small light goes on and off on the ceiling and steel circles rumble and hum.

I check out the men and the boys. They have no black lines or snakes that I can see. I take a breath of the ice air and sit, hugging my knees.

A woman with plastic gloves over her hands comes into the room.

'Marco,' she says in a voice that stretches.

I follow her into a side room with two red plastic chairs and a wooden table with a box of tissues in the middle of it.

'So what is your family name?' she asks.

I take a breath and say Mamá's words, 'Marco Fidelia.'

'Where's your mom, Marco?'

'They were going to kill me too,' I say.

I reach into my pocket and pull out the note that Mamá wrote. It looks like a tight cigarette and the woman takes a long time to smooth it out. She reads it, then goes out through the door. There are mirrored rectangles along the wall. I get up and go over to them, lift my T-shirt and turn to see the reflection of my back. There is an infection in the lower part like a yellow green country on the maps they had at school. I drop my T-shirt and bite my teeth as the fabric drags on the skin.

I was stirring beans when Mamá came for me. A soft fabric feeling on my back, then something hot and hard pressed there. The pain sucked and spread, a pain like my skin was ripping off. I screamed so loud I couldn't hear myself anymore and Mamá pulled the iron away, hissing, steaming and stinking. My skin was stuck to it along with the wavy ink lines of the snake.

Mamá's lips were blue, her face bone.

'You don't have to be like me,' she said.

She put her arms around me and we shook.

I sit down on one of the plastic chairs now and run my fingers along the wood. I take one of the tissues and tear a triangle pattern into it. Then I pull another one out and make a circle design.

The woman comes back in, and says, 'Follow me.'

She walks so fast I have to run to keep up. Her shoes squeal on the floor. We walk past doors with windows that have thin silver lines running through them. Then she holds open a door and doesn't come in with me.

'Hi Marco,' says a man with long hair pulled into a ponytail.

He tilts his head when he speaks. He is on a chair that spins, holding a piece of paper in front of him. He looks up at me, elbows on his far apart knees.

'So here's what we're gonna do: we're gonna take a look at your body to make sure you're in good health.'

'If you could go behind that screen and strip down to your underwear.'

Behind the screen, I pull off my T-shirt and take down the trousers. I drop the clothes as faraway from me as possible, on the floor beside a bin. I'm tired and sore and stooping. There is a trolley covered with blue paper and I lie down on my side.

'Okay if I come in now?' says the nurse or the doctor or whoever he is.

'Yes,' I say.

And the man comes in, and makes a sound like a slow, long draw on a cigarette.

'How did you get that, Marco?'

'Mmmm,' I say. 'They burnt me, said if I didn't leave town, they'd do it to my face too.'

'Did they ask you to be in the gang?'

'No,' I say.

Because how could this man with his soft fingers and his bendy voice understand that they don't give you a choice? How could he understand that Mamá had to make things easier for me? The man breathes out the invisible cigarette smoke. Then his plastic fingers are around the wound, pulling and peering.

'Ay!' I shout.

'I got a son your age,' he says. 'Cars are his thing. He knows all the different models. What do you like to do, Marco?'

The pain goes through me, something wet and cold on top of the minced up skin. Snakes, I think. But the only snakes I have left are the ones in my book.

'I like to read,' I say.

The man sticks something to my back like parcel tape.

'Well, you'll do for now,' he says. 'But we need to take care of that wound.'

He wraps a silver blanket around my shoulders and I crinkle back to the bright, white room.

I pull the book from my bag and lie down on my side. The woman, still with the yellow boy in her arms, bends and lifts my head. She puts a folded cardigan underneath me, lays me back down then pulls the book from my hands. I breathe deep and hear the rustle of the pages. The woman speaks so low that I barely hear her.

'*One of the biggest threats to the snake population is the destruction of their habitats by humans,*' she says.

'What's a habitat?' asks her little boy.

'Home,' the woman says.

I close my eyes and drift, letting my feet sink into the yellow grass. I kick the bottles and their faded labels. I pass wrinkled plastic bags and empty syringes. I walk until the grass turns green, a green to light up the dark. I breathe in the colour and feel the pink heat return to my cheeks.

A brown-scaled tail whips through the blades, but I run, pumping my legs fast. I overtake the snake and run on and on and on.

P.K. Read

P.K. Read is a French-American writer. She's published several short stories, written screenplays, worked for many years as a translator and had a surprising hit with a German-English film dictionary. She's never not working on another novel. She's a keen environmentalist, whisky enthusiast and a resigned gardener.

House of Doors

Skye had said they'd all be able to watch the beach from the train windows, but Owen was the only one looking, head against the glass, as the waves rolled in and families appeared out of nowhere and then zipped past into nothingness. Want to see what they were eating? Too late, they were already gone. Was that surfer catching a wave? Gone. In his head, it sounded like this, "Was that a? Gone. What was he? Gone. Wha? Gone. Hey? Gone."

"Hey, Sonic, you're doing it. Chatter alert." Skye had her going out makeup on even though it was early. Charles, the guy who had shown up at the door this morning, sat there with a lollipop look on his face. He'd been around before, though, like a mushroom Goomba who popped in and out of life.

Owen was home from school; San Diego didn't get rain or snow days but the occasional bomb threat sometimes livened up the schedule. Skye had rolled her eyes when she got the call. "It's just some kid playing a prank. It's grade school, for Christ's sake. A hoax." This to the school clerk who had contacted her. "Yeah, I know, there was a real one two years ago, yeah, good, can't take any chances thanks." She'd hung up and stared into space, then at Owen.

Now Owen was along for the ride. "Sonic," she said. "The chatter. And the legs."

Owen forced his legs to stop bopping, his mouth to stop flapping, did what Ms. Kaminski Call-Me-Cheryl told him to do: He took a deep breath in, breathed out slowly. Twice before speaking. "Okay. *Skye*."

Charles hung out a smile now like someone who just farted and hoped no one would notice. He had on a suit with a black T-shirt and loafers, no socks, cop show detective, West Coast version. CSI: Doucheville. Old, though, grey in his hair. "Hey, I used to do that, too. Talk out my thoughts out loud. Without noticing. No biggie."

Owen kept his lips zipped so no thoughts would leak out now. He really hated the Sonic name, and Skye knew it.

Charles said, "And then at some point I just stopped."

Like it was something awful.

Charles hitched up an even bigger idiot grin, and reached across to get the travel bag he'd put on the seat next to Owen. "Hey, listen buddy (who was he calling buddy, like Owen was some kind of dog, or a friend?), I picked something up for you on the way over this morning." He opened the bag, Skye's face rearranged. She didn't like surprises. At least, she never liked Owen's surprises, maybe she liked West Coast Cop's. She'd sounded chirpy when he'd called the previous night, Owen had only heard, "See you after nine, big C," and now Charles was here.

Out of Charles's bag came a box, and Christ-on-a-cracker as Skye liked to say, it was a brand-new Nintendo 3DS XL, some kind of pack with games pre-installed, Owen could see the pictures of Mario on the box from here.

"Uh." Skye reached out as if to take the box before it could be handed off to Owen, then withdrew her hand. "That's thoughtful, Charles. It's not, you know. It's not his birthday or anything. I mean, that's really nice."

This Charles guy had the power to override Call-Me-Cheryl's instructions about no games. Duly noted. Owen reached out, took the box, looked at Charles. "Wow. This is, this is sick. Wicked. Crash hot."

"Crash hot is good?" Charles looked uncertain.

"Yeah, crash hot is good." Owen upgraded Charles to CSI: Epic and started unpacking the box before Skye could stop him. Call-Me-Cheryl would spit her mint tea all over her flowing dress and handmade pendants if she saw him getting a handheld like this, she'd called it his 'crack equivalent' when she'd banned all video games just the previous week, but then, she said the same thing about sugar. The space between Owen's eyes thrilled with anticipatory buzz.

"Even had time to charge it up already for you, buddy." Buddy my ass, but Owen just smiled down at the screen as Super Smash Brothers loaded its glorious goodness. "It says age ten and over for the game bundle, and you're?"

"Nine."

"Well, but a grown-up nine. So."

"Sonic." Skye was leaning in towards him in a way that sometimes meant a rough pinch on the arm but this time it was just her we-have-company smile. "What do you say?"

"We say, thank you very much, Charles. This is so great!" Charles had just made the jump from a Goomba to a Yoshi. Maybe even better.

"Wow, I'm glad you like it, Owen. I hoped you would."

"I love it." He meant it. He loved it. Right then, he loved it more than Skye, or food, or that stolen pocketknife he had under his mattress at home. And he would be playing it to pieces before Skye or Call-Me-Cheryl could take it away from him.

He fired up the DS and let its two-screen 3D absolution wash over him. The two weeks without gaming fell away, a shed skin. Smash Brothers had Sonic the Hedgehog as a character, as if Owen would ever pick that loser as his avatar just because he was super speedy and could curl up like a hedgehog. Big deal. Zach called him Sploid and so did everyone else at school. Exploding droid, he knew what it meant. But Zach also sometimes let Owen sit with his posse said he always played Ike from Fire Emblem. Owen picked Ike. He was already hip deep in smashing when he heard voices penetrating the battle.

"Hey, Sonic, we're going to go look for the smoking car. Sonic?"

He looked up. They were both standing. "Uh-huh."

"Keep an eye on my bag, right, buddy?"

"Sure."

"Sonic. No getting off or anything without me, right?"

"Obviously, Skye."

Skye made her cute company pouty face that actually meant she was angrier than she looked. "Okay. We'll be back soon."

He was back in the battle again, only hearing a vague whisper above him, Charles's voice, "It only seemed fair, my others have one," but Skye was already pulling him down the aisle and they were out of earshot.

Mario & Co. beckoned. Owen switched seats with Charles's bag. The light reflecting off the ocean was causing glare on the screens.

The Mission San Juan Capistrano was emptier than the other time he'd been there, but the garden was still a heap of floral confusion. He flinched as a bee passed, the memory of the sting from last time still sharp. A couple of old people were sitting on stone benches, ooh-ing and aah-ing over the amazing beauty of this ruin.

"How do you like it," Charles said.

"It's okay." It was an old pile of dried mud, what was to like? A bunch of priests had lived there, then they didn't, then they did, and now they didn't again. History. It all seemed pretty pointless.

"So, you've got your tour headset, if we lose sight of each other, you just finish up the tour and I'll find you, right?" Skye's hand on her hip, her selfie pose. She looked like a model. Well, she was a model, sometimes. Sometimes Zach's friends hit Owen because they said he was too pretty. The worst Zach ever did was call him Sploid.

"It says fourth grade level, is that okay for you?" Charles looked worried, like it was somehow up to him.

"I'm in fourth grade."

"Excellent!"

Sure enough, by the time the audio tour had gotten him to the Soldiers Barracks, Owen looked up – Skye and Charles were gone. No problem. The Barracks had wooden cots and a couple of tables, bleak as hell if you had to live there in the 1800s. It was the same audio tour they'd handed out on the school trip a couple of months earlier. They'd come on a bus instead of the train, Skye had obviously forgotten or maybe she'd never even known about it. Owen had gotten a B+ on that test, easy enough when the questions were about Native Americans and smallpox and wars. The good stuff. The corner between a cool stone wall and one of the cots at the back of the display was ideal for digging deep into level-busting the new game.

He blasted through the first level, easy as falling asleep, like Skye said except that falling asleep was actually hard sometimes but he knew what she meant. Easy as falling down, now there was something that was easy.

How was he supposed to get up that last set of suspended platforms in the Arena Ferox? The Mission audio tour had run out, static coming out of the headset, not enough to drown out the boopity-boop of the 3DS, which he had turned down so no one would hear it, a rookie mistake for clandestine gaming.

His beefy Ike jumped the platform, dropped down, jumped again, but this time when he dropped, it felt like Owen himself was physically dropping. Like, that his body was dropping and there was louder noise and after a moment, he looked up and realized it was a non-game earthquake. A big one.

Owen felt a cold rush of real life. The walls, the stone wall against his back and all the others, were moving and making noise like the ocean. A whooshing. He heard a scream from outside. The church bells clanked out an ugly warning and Owen remembered what to do. Duck and cover. Duck and cover, just like in the drills at school.

He pushed his body as hard as he could into the gap between floor and cot, but it was too narrow. He threw himself over to a nearby table, jammed his shoulders down and held his knees. The old pots that were on the wall near the end of the room crashed down and rolled around, one rolled towards him with an iron drum thump, like it was aiming for him.

A couple more screams and the pots banged around and then it was over. A final pot fell to the floor. It got all quiet, and then someone was screaming again. It was his name in two different voices.

"Owen!" The voice that wasn't his mother's must have been Charles', it had a pleasing manly boom and concern to it. "Owen!" Having a father yell his name in concern wasn't something Owen had ever considered, but now it occurred to him that it could be a nice element to have in life.

He was listening to his name echo around when they found him, still under the table.

Skye pulled him out from his spot and hugged him harder than he could remember. The streaky trails through her makeup made her look prettier, she didn't seem to notice that she was crying.

"Jesus Christ, baby, I couldn't see you anywhere!"

Another arm and another smell manifested and it was Charles, his arms around both of them. "That was a big one!" Like a family, almost.

Cold air against his chest when the two adults pulled away, and something hot in his hand. He looked down. It was the 3DS, and before he had a chance to think about it, he wanted to play it again more than anything else.

"Owen," said Charles, "that little table wouldn't have done you much good. A solid doorway is always better." There were three tables in the room, two big ones with benches, and this small one that had a pitcher and basin on the top, dusty white porcelain, closest to the corner where he'd been gaming.

Owen shrugged. The doorway, arched and with a heavy wooden door permanently thrown open, was all the way across the room. "At school they say 'duck and cover'."

"Yeah, but underneath something that'll do you some good." Charles smiled like this was a good joke and now Skye smiled, too. She was dabbing at her cheeks with the back of her hands.

"No more wandering off today, Owen." An unaccustomed lightness to Skye's hand on his shoulder.

At home he was only allowed to watch cartoons online because then Skye could check which ones he'd watched on the history. One of Call-Me-Cheryl's bright ideas. It didn't stop him from watching much because Skye never knew the names of any of the shows. As long as he avoided anything from the no-watch list, he was fine.

He'd come across one once, a Roadrunner cartoon. Like most Roadrunner cartoons, it was less about the Roadrunner and more about the coyote chasing him, Wile E. Coyote, and how he got smashed up trying to catch the bird. The one Owen remembered now was when the coyote tried to get the roadrunner to eat earthquake pellets that would cause the bird to shake itself to death, a snappy idea until the coyote took a bunch of the pills himself to see whether they worked. Oh yeah, they worked. A tremor would start in one foot, run up the coyote's leg, and within seconds his whole body would be engulfed in wild jitters, replete with bells and sirens, almost like a real earthquake. And the coyote would rattle uncontrollably, shattering anything in his path, smashing rocks and cliffsides and roads and his own teeth and then his own body before the shaking stopped and he could gather the pieces of himself together.

Owen knew the feeling. Inner quakes were nothing like the earthquake today. Inner quakes were scarier because there were no tables or doorways.

The restaurant where they went for lunch was supposed to look like Italy because of the white walls and all the dried pasta in jars and the garlic smell. The spaghetti from the kid's menu was red sauce and white noodles and that was about all it was. Skye and Charles had ordered grown-up food full of fish and mushrooms but neither of them were eating much. Their wine glasses kept getting refilled, along with Owen's diet Coke, another of the crack equivalents, even if it was supposed to be sugar-free.

Skye said she was going out for a smoke and Charles excused himself to go to the bathroom while she was gone. Owen was able to push aside the plate of so-called food and work on getting past the Arena Ferox. Time was nothing more than a floating platform and then his Ike burst forth in muscular victory, into a Balloon Fight level that featured lightning clouds that hit his Ike and sent him tumbling into the water below, where he was dragged to his doom by Balloon Fight fish. It was a mess.

A real world rumbling noise rose up around him and his body was electrified because it was another earthquake. He tried to dive beneath the table but there were legs there, legs and hands in his way, and he realized that the legs and hands were beating the underside of the table. Then the rumbling was replaced by laughter. Skye and Charles were back, Skye's hair like it had been in a wind storm while she was out smoking, same as when they'd come back from the smoking car on the train. They were both looking at him and laughing, people at the tables around them were looking and laughing like he was a sideshow freak.

"I told you, buddy, doors, not tables," Charles said. The table had already been cleared and Owen didn't remember anyone taking away the plates. "But they have to be exterior doors. You know, doors that lead outside."

"Don't be angry, it was just a joke," Skye said. Her hand was on Charles's but she moved it away when Owen glanced at it. She reached up to smooth her hair. "Hey, Charles, what do you think, if a door is the safest place to be, then you just need a door in every wall and you're all set. Huh, Sonic?"

"Jails." Owen thought of more places with doors in all the walls. "Schools. Clinics."

"No," Skye shook her head. "Outside doors. A house with doors in every wall? There would always be a safety door, and you could always just walk right out through any wall. You could leave whenever you wanted."

They were at the train station. Charles was leaving on a train to Los Angeles, Owen and Skye were waiting for a train back down to San Diego.

He'd gone back to the Balloon Fight while they'd been waiting for the train with Charles.

"What did you tell the others?" Skye was saying above his head, she said The Others like they were aliens who might be on the lookout for Charles's whereabouts.

"Told them my flight got into LA at six tonight. Course, that was before, you know." He meant Owen being there instead of at school. "No biggie, I'll just tell her I caught an earlier flight back."

Charles's face suddenly appeared in front of Owen's. "Hey. Owen. Glad you like the game."

"I love it. Thanks."

"Cool. Crash hot." Which was a stupid thing to say. Charles reached out a finger and put it on Owen's chin. There was a small indentation there, 'butt chin' Zach called it on the bad days, and Charles put his forefinger right on it, then put the same forefinger on the much deeper cleft in his own chin, which had just a small shading of grey and black bristle starting to show. "We're chin partners. Nice to see you, kid."

Whatever that meant.

Then he and Skye were talking again and the train pulled in and they kissed and he was gone. Owen busted Balloon Fight and was well into an epic level featuring a floating island, he was sure he could beat this level if he could just concentrate. That last parent-teacher meeting had the teachers and Call-Me-Cheryl rattling on to Skye about avoiding 'setbacks', about 'progress made' and 'improvements'. Once they were on the train, or at the latest, once they were home, Skye would remember Call-Me-Cheryl's instructions and take away the handheld.

Skye was saying something, her hand floated over the game and he missed a jump and lost his last life. "Hey, Sonic, train's coming in just a couple of minutes. Let's put that away until we get on the train, okay." Her voice got the edge it had when guys like Charles weren't around.

He pushed reset and started the level again. "I can just finish this in a sec', Mom." Now that Charles was gone, he could call her by her least favorite name.

"Sonic."

"Owen, *Mom*."

Now her face was in front of him. "We had a good day. Let's not do this."

He kept playing. "Do what? Mom?" He did his flat robot Sploid voice.

"Listen." Her hand was on his shoulder now, hard, and her voice was snaky quiet. She was good at that, the whole velvet glove act of looking like she was a nice, concerned mom while she was pinching him hard enough to bruise. "I swear to god? Owen? Do not go where you are going right now? You were barely polite to our friend the whole day."

"Your friend, Mom." The Sploid voice drove her crazy. It drove everyone crazy.

"I swear. Our friend. Dammit, Owen. I will get on this train and leave you here."

He shrugged off her hand and pressed reset. She tried to take away the handheld, he held on tight. And he could feel it rising in him, the rattling, like earthquake pills and nothing like a real earthquake, it started in his feet and rose and washed over him like a fast-rising tide pushing everything ahead of it and he was in it, teeth shattering, shattering everything around him. That loud screaming on the wind was his own, he could hear it but didn't know how to make it stop.

And then it started to ebb, like it always did, sooner or later. He was a hedgehog curled on the platform, wrung out, his face wet with angry tears, several puzzled faces peering down at him from the stalks of long legs. Not one of them was Skye. Skye was gone. He thrust himself upright. Two old ladies in matching pink sweatshirts frowned at him. One said, "Aren't you a bit too old for that, young man?" but he ignored her and looked around for Skye.

The Surfliner train was in the station, he ran along the side of the train, and then he saw her Barbie blond, shiny hair from behind. She was on the train, sitting in a seat, not looking around, looking straight ahead.

"Skye, Skye!" he yelled out. He was right in front of her, she had to be able to hear him, but she didn't look down. He banged on the wall of the train. "Mom! Skye!"

A whistle blew and the train doors all slammed shut. Owen was screaming but Skye didn't deign to glance. The train made a slight jerk forward, then came to rest like it had decided not to leave, after all.

A man in a uniform was flying down the platform in his direction. He pulled up short in front of Owen. "Son, what you are doing! You got to step back from the train!"

"My mom's on the train, I need to get on! She's right there, in the smoking car." Why did he say that? It seemed like a good thing to say. It was because Skye was holding an unlit cigarette in her hands.

He pointed up at Skye, who was looking down at them now. She adjusted her face into a look of surprise, and waved for Owen to join her. Maybe she hadn't heard him, after all.

"There's no smoking on Amtrak trains, kid, that's just a regular car."

The train conductor was leaning out the window at the front of the train, the stationmaster gave him a wave, and walked Owen to the nearest door. He opened it with a key, lifted Owen up into the train, and walked him down to Skye. She smiled at Owen, at the stationmaster.

"My God, Owen, I saw you get on the train? You almost got left behind!" She pulled him towards her, taking his hand so firmly that her nails dug into his palm. To the conductor, "My goodness, sir, thank you so much! That was a close call!"

The stationmaster tipped his hat, and exited the train. The door snapped shut. The train lurched, then started to move. Skye released Owen's hand, dropped the smile and looked out the window, fiddled the unlit cigarette like it was a poker chip in search of the next best bet.

"If we sit on the other side, we can watch the ocean going back down," he said. Skye huffed once, ignored him.

His game was still in his hand, but Owen sat for a moment, still trying to breathe in and out from the earthquake attack and all the yelling. His throat hurt.

There was a good chance Skye couldn't get any angrier today. Even if someone traced the bomb threat back to Skye's cell phone, used very briefly while she'd been in the shower that morning, she probably couldn't get any angrier than she was right now. And even if she did, well, there was the usual reset. Call-Me-Cheryl, or whoever the next Call-Me-Name turned out to be, was always on his side.

He fired up the 3DS, and plunged into the floating Battlefield. He twisted himself so the light reflecting off the ocean wouldn't cause glare on his screens.

Derek Routledge

Derek Routledge was born in York and lives in Wales. His poetry has been published in *Poetry Wales* and the *Anglo-Welsh Review*. His short story *Key Under the Mat* was adapted for BBC Radio 4 Woman's Hour in 2005. *The War on Television* won the 2006 Sheffield Theatres' Cued Up runner up prize, selected by Sam West, for a performed rehearsed reading at the Crucible. It also won the 2006 Drama Association of Wales Best Play Award for youth cast, published by DAW 2010. *Birthplace* won a 2011 Rhys Davies Short Story runner up prize. He is currently completing a novel selected for the spring 2015 Curtis Brown Online Novel-Writing course.

Dance Of The
Light Deprived Children

We are in the big room upstairs. in our underpants. with our goggles on.

and i go shivery when i think about switch on. and i like the name of it Ultraviolet. and i roll it around on my tongue and say it to myself. and it makes me think of flowers.

because there is a name. for a flower with colour same. though i can't remember. can't think of flowers easy today. because it is so cold. twenty below outside. bozz the caretaker said who drives the rusty van here. it might not start. the roads are bad. we will be lucky. if we make it. but we did.

with snow chains.

and i think of it as funny what they call it. when we all undress together. there are six of us here. my best friend Anto away. and to comfort me i use the whole words they call it. i learned inside my head: Ultraviolet Light Bath. Ultraviolet Light Bath.

miss j comes in again. through the door at the far end. with all the paint scratched off. but left without any new paint. maybe because it got forgot.

i am glad she has not. gone anywhere.

she stays with us. and talks with big nurse. who is strict and stretches her uniform. all over so it might burst. even more when she bends over. tugs at the lamp. tuts tuts. clicks the switch again. and it does not come on.

the doctor is not here. the one miss j talks to. he fixed it once before.

sometimes i think maybe big nurse. will light up. instead of the lamp. but then i know that not possible. she is not someone who can. an adult who never ever will. who only says each time:

be still. all of you.

stop moving.

we are still. three boys. three girls.

boys wear underpants. girls wear bra things when older. but we all wait in just our pants. the Light will make it good. when we are older.

we need to grow up strong. the Light does things. when it gives us our bath. If we don't have it we will not be right. all sorts.

inside our. bodies. minds.

i'm shivery. but not because the word on my tongue.

the room so cold. iron radiators that go tink. burn dust smells. but not today. the town hall boiler not working. for two days.

bozz told miss j. in the van when we set off. she looked worried. asked him to wait a moment.

she went back. inside the school for something. then got in the van again. told him get us here safe. i don't like it that she is worried. but i like she worries about us. it makes me feel safe.

tell my mother. she nods. strokes the top of my head. once with her hand. but does not say anything.

miss j has a smile that everyone likes. even when we do maths.

the most daylight we had. last month. two hours and thirty five minutes. she gets us to add them up. we do a chart. it is on the wall.

i find it hard. i like singing songs best. and memorying poems. miss j says they are songs. some of them i don't get. but like the sounding. she puts a record on. with someone saying words.

the shivers make my skin bump. like the leg of a chicken. which is dead.

through my goggles i see it turn. we keep hands behind backs. stand still as told. but it is hard. i want to move my arms. my skin has bumps.

i want to press them down. with my fingers. but i keep still.

the lamp will not work. it has done this before.

miss j on her knees. she tries to help.

big nurse pulls at the cable. pinches the switch. with her fat thumb and finger. there is no power. or some but not enough. the lamp is bright and needs a lot.

it eats it. to feed us.

the girl stood next to me new. i do not know her. she is shaking.

a sound in her throat. her head moves like a horse's. with goggles on.

big nurse will shout. if i move. i am afraid i would wee. it is hard to comfort girls. especially in underpants. i clasp my fingers tighter.

miss j looks round. at us. like we are like discovery. something new.

like never seen before. like she taught us. about people. who sailed to new lands.

when they first saw. after a long time.

her mouth opens. she gets up off her knees.

my ears hurt. i do not hear her voice. try to think. but too hard. like my head has gone solid.

miss j is in the corner. she talks whilst she gets something. a big black disk. out of white paper. with a shhh noise.

there is a wooden box. a grille like a car front. the lid opens. two brown buttons like snail shells. she moves them. puts the black disc inside.

frowns. in that way of hers. waits.

then smiles. there is power.

– children get ready!

she claps and it breaks the cold. a crack in ice.

– vinyl is here! to the rescue!

big nurse stares. miss j waves at her.

a loud hissing noise. i am afraid. because i think vinyl may be fierce. when he comes. i look around. but cannot see him.

– no-no-no it is alright! miss j calls. vinyl is good!

music fills the room. hits me in the stomach.

but not in a bad way. it makes us. all six.

smile at once.

– move around! move round! get warm children!"

we break out of line. at the edge of the carpet. move into the middle. pass each other near. nearly crash but do not. a space appears. like magic. wherever we decide. and again and again. when we move.

one space.

to another.

it is in her throat. the girl next to me. who was shaking. her mouth opens beneath her goggles. lets out under the music.

laughter.

and then mine. bubbles out. everyones does.

in space. each second. we change. decide to go. somewhere else.

– that's it!

miss j claps in time.

– get warm!

and then the doctor here. at the painty peely door. one hand on it.

and laughs.

everything is funny. he is going. to paint everything. a bright colour.

he has just decided. and miss j going too. his smile picks her.

makes her turn. smile back.

big nurse by the lamp. still hunched. still will not work.

she turns where miss j looks. she straightens up. pulls at her uniform. it will not straighten stuck. on her roly poly bits. which i am scared to think of.

she might read inside my head. see what is in it. tell me off.

shout.

we are not still. It works. we dance to music. throw ourselves round.

we laugh. warm works in our bodies. we move faster. the doctor laughs.

he walks over to big nurse.

her mouth moves and she tells him. waits his order. the music to stop. but he does not. he stoops down. miss j watches.

she looks over at us. then him again. like big nurse not there.

he pulls the cord. turns the switch.

i want the music. to go on forever. the others do too. I can tell.

i want bozz to come in. see us and laugh. like he can sometimes in a good mood. i want my mother to see me dance. i think of the word and roll it on my tongue again like miss j taught us Ultraviolet Ultraviolet... Ultra –

and then the whole world lights up.

as if the moon come in day-time.

makes friends in the room with the sun.

 which we hardly get to see.

we are bathing growing just like the slogan says.

the Light Bath. goes with music. is part of it.

and then nobody can believe.

the doctor takes big nurse's arm.

pulls her away from the Lamp.

not just so the beam not on her and just on us for safe.

for her to move.

with him.

big nurse with the doctor.

begins to dance around.

miss j claps her hands.

laughter.

as we whirl in our pants.

the best Light Bath ever.

big Nurse

smiles.

for the first time.

Anto should be.

here to see.

the doctor smile.

turn to miss j.

the happiest.

she has been.

since she taught us.

a word on my tongue.

says how.

but I cannot think it.

so I say again all in one which I learned inside my head which I love Ultraviolet Ultraviolet Ultraviolet Light Bath Ultraviolet Light Bath Ultraviolet Ult

A picture, he says. One he will never forget.

He laughs down the line, says the Nurse moved surprisingly well. But he cannot – will not – believe that someone with such girth is called Sylvia.

She laughs. "Sylvia's are svelte, like you," he says. "If they frown, it is like you, to die for, incredible." She laughs again, and chides him. Tells him not to ever upset the Nurse. Who she's scared of.

– No need, he says.

His voice different.

She does not ask. Wants only to be alone with him. Not have anything else in her head. Always, he takes her somewhere else.

He will be over soon. When they've finished off.

– Ahh... It's been so busy.

Then he has to go. The line clicks dead.

She listens to the purring. Holds the wall-mounted receiver away from her ear like a shell picked up on a beach. There in the narrow hall of her one-bedroomed flat. She replaces it on the hook and takes off her clothes.

She is tired from the day, the kids. But the thought of him overrides.

She smiles to herself. She stays underneath for a long time. Lets the water cascade. Takes one, on her finger. Tastes it. Millions of droplets down her body.

Indulgent. She will save more tomorrow.

Images of the intensity of the beam return. As she dries herself.

Their trust in their little pants, whilst they waited for the lamp to be fixed. Stock still at attention which she hates.

Thank God, they got it going. Or he did. He is brilliant.

At least it was not a Power Cut; they would have had to cancel altogether.

And thanks to good old Vinyl, who came to the rescue and never went away. She said this to the kids accidentally in a lesson. The first time she played them anything.

– Good old Vinyl... He never went away.

They began to ask questions. About what he looked like.

Some of them were very frightened. It took her a moment to realise.

That they thought she was referring to a real person.

– Is he big?

– A monster?

– Does he live near?

– Where?

– Is he coming into our classroom?

She had to explain; reassure. It was as if they were talking about Grendel. Like she'd read Beowulf to them or something.

And then it turned out, they were. The teacher before her who went mad had read it out to them.

They thought Vinyl was related.

She made a lesson out of it. They drew their own version of a friendly creature called Vinyl who was lots of fun. Who got everybody up on their feet, moving and laughing, keeping warm.

It was the best they had been. She learned a lot.

How the dark affected them. Got inside their minds.

How music – old scratchy music on worn out discs played on discarded equipment – opened up something she did not realise was there. Deep beneath. Letting it, out so something else can take its place.

Something good.

When he arrives, there is not much talk.

They are hungry. They do not get out of the tiny hall of her flat. He drops his bag.

Against the wall, her legs round him. The ancient lampshade knocked into a carousel of lights on his face – ecstatic. Crumpled clothes together, the dull carpet, cracked walls filled and painted whilst she thought about him the summer he arrived.

A hidden day collides. Talk without words; demands, pleas. The push uncompromising to take what they've kept in shadow and out of sight.

After the first wave, in the acoustic on the floor, breaths together fast. He props himself on an elbow. Looks down at her and smiles. A game they play; who will speak first.

– Food

Some prepared, she says. Glad to lose.

He looks at her but still does not speak. They both want more. He strokes her breasts, kisses her nipples. The bedroom; she is about to lead him there to where she fucks him and he looks up at her and tells her to never stop.

– What?

At the table he takes expensive wine out of his bag.

He loves the food, everything. Compliments, until she tells him to shut up.

– Promotion, he says

Immediate departure, end of the week. His replacement ready. An apartment in the capital only dreamt of

– Look.

They've sent him pictures on his phone. His breathing close to hers.

She nods. Makes noises of approval.

It is not enough.

– What's wrong?

This is good news, he tells her. He's had a bad day. Come on for Christ's sake.

– What day?

– None, he says. That's the point. There aren't any here. We're leaving!

– What happened?

– Kid.

– What kid?

– Died.

– Which?

– Any kid...I don't know...

– One of ours?...Mine?

– They're all fucking yours!

– Name...His name?

– I don't...An something...Ant...What does it ma –

– How?

– Bones...They'd disintegrated more than…and Hey...Wait! Wait!

In the night, she wakes and gets up.

She moves as quietly as possible...He sleeps on.

Something has disturbed her beneath. A dream, lost somewhere. Deep in the dark.

A sound? Coming from far away; calling to her.

She leaves the bedroom. Goes down the hall.

The child is still fast asleep.

To the living room, the window.

She rubs at the glass. Tastes her fingertips. Moisture a nectar on her lips.

Outside the single allocated light flares its weak offering. Beneath it, she sees. Their movements her trace for the source of the sound. The two of them together, hand in hand in release and delight.

The music they dance to from far away. The voices shouting over. A name?..Their names?

They were friends but she cannot remember the names now.

Nose to the glass...Closer.

She jumps back.

"Vinyl!...Vinyl!..VINYL HE'S COMING!"

Penny Simpson

Penny Simpson completed an MA in the Theory and Practice of Human Rights at Essex University, and now divides her time between further academic studies and prose. She has published two novels, *The Banquet of Esther Rosenbaum* and *The Deer Wedding*, and one collection of short stories. Her novella *In Wolf Wolf* has been shortlisted for the 2015 Novella Award. She has been the recipient of an Arts Council of Wales New Writer's Bursary, an Arts Council Travel Bursary, and a Hawthornden Fellowship. She is currently working on a new collection of short stories.

Marbles

Here's where it begins, Magda thinks, a fight to the death. She is the oldest by a matter of minutes, counted off on a stopwatch by Uncle Erhard; close on her kicking heels, her shadow sister, Bibi. The twins have pale, heart-shaped faces. When they stand face to face, it's like staring in a mirror. They clench fists, and circle each other. Uncle Erhard is teaching them to box.

"Remember, if you lead with your chin it makes you easy to punch."

He looks from one to the other, his own face a blank. Which is which? No one can tell, except for the twins. Mama brushes back their curly red hair to find the clue: a splotchy mole that lies far up on Magda's forehead. The tell-tale mark of distinction. She is the best, the most resilient in the long drawn out battles between sisters born just minutes apart. A shadow sister is like a big, heavy overcoat which Magda kicks in the dust so it won't weigh her down.

"I know what you're thinking, every second of every minute, " Bibi says.

Magda resents her taunt. This is how it begins, finding a place where there are no mirror faces to scare her, or make her angry. A place where she is Magda and there are no hidden surprises waiting to hit her, like a pea-in-the-pod sister who runs round a corner and sends her flying, and, for one, painful minute, she thinks she has run, bang slap, into herself.

Uncle Erhard makes infrequent visits to the front parlour to see the family. He adjusts his plumed hat and salutes the tea table. He's fighting a war, says Mama. The war began when the twins turned eight. Uncle Erhard presented them with bracelets of coloured beads to mark the occasion, but the twins preferred the shiny coins he wore on a coloured ribbon on his uniform. The mystery is: Uncle Erhard fights, but he doesn't get recriminations pouring down on his head like a tumble of mouldy old leaves. Magda watches him, alert to every tic and twitch. He sits up straight, even when he drinks from a bone china tea cup. His moustache drips tea on his knee-high boots. Bibi traces its fall with the tips of her fingers, until he swats her away like a nuisance fly. There isn't much talking with Uncle Erhard at the table. When he takes his leave, he makes another crisp salute and clicks his heels. He doesn't seem able to leave the military parade ground, even in a room decked out with lace antimacassars and half-dead potted plants.

What Magda knows is this: they are his bastards. So says Milan who comes to clean the drains at the house before the winter rains begin. But Magda is no one's anything, neither fish nor fowl, nor ugly, little bastard. She kicks Milan on the shins – a solo victory for once – and runs six times round the walled garden in triumph. When a bomb falls in the village, the twins are shut away in the cellar. Mama stays upstairs, rolling her collection of lace into tiny parcels. The family photographs are concealed under cushions. The bomb falls, and the house swings like an acrobat before righting itself. Gaps open between the floorboards, and the twins look up into the room where tea is taken. They watch Mama sway too. She looks like the bullrushes down by the river, knocked about by the wind, every which way. What happens next, they're not sure, but one morning she's no longer sat by the parlour table and the tea cups are all cracked. The twins start a new game: Where is everybody? They spy round broken walls, and learn to recognise the siren which warns them to take cover. One night, the house receives a direct hit; down it goes in a tumble of bricks. The twins watch from the other end of the walled garden.

"How did they know where to find the house in the dark?" Bibi asks.

Magda has no idea, but she isn't going to admit it. They head for the road that leads to the village, but it has been transformed into a river of gluey mud, pinpricked with the bodies of dead animals. Magda spots Milan's piebald horse, its guts laid out alongside its open belly, like a string of pink sausages. It is hard walking along a road that is full of dead dogs and goats, their bloated bellies transformed into nets of buzzing flies. The twins fight their way through, eyes and mouths closed, and their fingers wedged in their ears. Magda knows that if a fly gets inside them, it will lay eggs and in nine months time they will burst open and their bellies will be buzzing like those of the dead goats. Bibi bursts into tears. Magda also knows that Uncle Erhard lives in the city, because Mama occasionally talked about her old life there and how they once danced until dawn and she wore out a pair of gold brocade shoes. No knowing where that story came from really. Magda makes up stories all the time, like the story about the fly eggs, but this one might be true. Bibi hunches over her belly, crying because she's hungry and she's tired and she can't walk with her eyes shut, and her fingers stuck in her ears. Magda opens her eyes, and blinks, and there in front of her, as if conjured by a spell, is a cart, driven by a man who looks like a troll.

"Take us to where Mama danced her shoes into holes," she says.

The troll laughs. He's barefoot.

"High hopes is what you need. Not much else left, truth telling."

He's not exaggerating. The twins watch open-mouthed (all flies forgotten) as the cart heaves its way into the outskirts of the city. Broken down apartment blocks lie every which way, obliterating what were once straight-as-a-die boulevards. Magda and Bibi jump down from the cart and run as fast as they can in case the troll demands money. Running into the wind which is tinged with the scent of about-to-fall snow. It sucks out what little breath is left in their tired, shaking bodies. Somewhere, between the Road of Flies and the City of Black Bricks, Bibi loses her voice. Magda pulls open her sister's mouth, thinking it might be blocked with dead flies, but there is nothing there, nothing at all, not even the husks of unspoken words. She hugs Bibi, terrified by her uncharacteristic silence. Her sister takes her hand. They turn round, slowly, like the hands on a damaged clock face, trying to absorb something from the chaos around them. A billboard, advertising face powder, has been propped up against a lump of wall; an upturned chair stands next to it. The twins watch fascinated as the chair scuttles towards them. A man crouches underneath. Snail Man, thinks Magda, and smiles. The man smiles back. No teeth, just black gums and lips cracked with blisters. "Safe as houses, safe as crocodiles," he says. His laugh is all cracked up and discordant, like the sound of water forcing its way out of a pipe.

Snail Man lives under his chair, because he thinks it is his only protection against bombs, stray dogs and hunger. This is what he tells Magda one night. He shuffles up and down the street with his chair on his back, drinking from puddles and chewing on weeds. Magda treats Snail Man like a pet. Bibi is less sure. Since she's lost her voice, she seems to have lost something of her old fighting self. No longer a mirror opposite, more a foggy reflection, like the one Magda sees reflected back at her in the tailor shop where she scavenges for clothes. Probably just as well, because she knows her hair has started to fall out and her teeth too. Bibi collects their teeth, hiding them away in a small jar.

At the tailor's, Magda finds two, thick flannel shirts, hardly even singed. One for her, one for Bibi. She takes a wool jacket for Snail Man, but he refuses to wear it. If he puts the jacket on, he will have to let go of his chair. The twins don't argue. They wrap themselves inside the jacket when night comes, taking a sleeve each, and tucking up like cherries on a stem. Magda remembers the cherry trees in the walled garden where they used to play. She hasn't thought about home for a long time, and it makes her cry. Bibi doesn't understand, and it's only then that Magda realises her sister can't steal her thoughts anymore; she has lost her shadow self.

Magda stays alert to the threat of further loss. Danger is the packs of stray dogs who strip bodies to the bone, right there, in the middle of the street. Snail Man rocks and cries under his unholy steeple, whilst the twins sit up on a window ledge and hope their combined weight won't dislodge the brick and see them tumble down like Humpty Dumpty, straight into the jaws of the starving dogs. They improvise a home on the first-floor of the tailor's shop, constructing a tent with blankets to replace the non-existent walls. Snail Man stays rooted to the earth, rocking backwards and forwards under his chair. His terrible smell keeps the dogs at bay. His fingers twist and turn, tangling up with each other; they move as fast as an aeroplane, as fast as the twins, who run through the streets, losing words and their teeth like coins from a torn pocket.

Food is a dead bird found in a gutter. Magda makes a fire, using a tinder box and matches stolen from a derelict she found frozen to death, in Turmstrasse. "No use crying over spilt milk," she says, but it's been a long time since they drank from a cow, any of them. Days pass; the twins' hair falls out in shaggy tufts. "A woman's glory," Uncle Erhard used to say, taking the porcelain pins from Mama's hair, and wrapping her long tresses round his arms. Mama washed her hair in water scented with marigold petals. The twins rub at their nits and chew up their remaining strands of hair, washing it with spittle as they go. Every once in a while, Magda bites their fingernails down into a rough-and-ready shape, the two of them curled up on the ground, face-to-face. A vagrant, wearing a decrepit frock coat and torn, pin-striped trousers, makes regular visits. He watches the Snail Man, as if he were a cinema newsreel come to life. The stranger taps his head with his fingers, but it's not a salute.

"Doolally-tap, I shouldn't wonder," he says. "It happens, sometimes. Sane as a pineapple one minute, then fizz, bang wallop, and that's your marbles scattered to the four ends of the earth."

Magda imagines marbles bursting out of Snail Man's head and bouncing off down the street to wherever the ends of the world might be. She pities him because his memories are lost for ever, sunk inside those wayward, glass bubbles. She takes to wearing an old hat she finds abandoned on top of a decapitated garden statue. If the hat is on her head, she is invincible. Her memories are buried deep inside her, so they can't be let loose. She tries to explain this to Bibi, but she's lying on her side in the gutter, sniffling.

Her stomach is bad. She can only eat so many nettles, before she starts vomiting and sweating.

"What we need is a cup of tea, or better still a cup of hot chocolate."

Magda puts on her hat. Walking keeps her from ending up like Snail Man, or Bibi. This much she knows: it all began with the terrible fighting and the sense of being suffocated by a body double who read and stole her every thought. Now, it's different. No more stealing, except for the things she finds on her walks. Her journeys are mapped by the places where she buries her stolen booty, a tin of sardines here, a one-sleeved jumper there. She lies awake at night, staring up under her hat, and imagines herself on the move, checking each precious token of another, richer life. Bibi prefers to sleep. Magda used to collect butterfly chrysalises in a glass jar lined with leaves. She thinks her sister must be like one of those husks; one day, she will wake up and burst into a new life.

In the meantime, she waits. Day after day, until the frosts clear and the sun comes out, just like it did in the country. Blistering, hot suns that cook up the dead, like so many fancy cuts on a restaurant menu. One morning, the vagrant swaggers by; he carries a pomander, which he sniffs at rather ostentatiously when he passes by Snail Man. The pomander is a child's rubber ball, pinpricked with faded flowers. He says he has come bearing gifts, a pocketful of silk scarves, which he has knotted together and brandishes, like a conjuror.

Snail Man chews his scarf into ribbons; Magda decides to wear hers pirate-style. She ties Bibi's into a turban to cover up what is left of her hair.

"The war is over," the vagabond says.

"Who won?"

"God knows. And good luck to him if he ever finds out."

He presents the pomander to Magda. Flowers are all well and good, she thinks, but she's hungry and Bibi won't wake up. She heads to the checkpoint by the cathedral and finds it abandoned, except for a hollow faced man who plays a squawky accordion and croaks out a bitter-sweet song: "I know where the angels go." Magda doesn't join in. She's listening in to a conversation behind her and learns that fresh fish is on sale, from a cart that has just parked up in Eislebenstrasse. Off Magda trots, digging up a few of her treasures along the way to barter for food.

She discovers the fish isn't the freshest by a long chalk, but at least it is fish. She trades cods heads (including the eyes) for a packet of ivory buttons and a portable chess set. Magda thinks about how she might cook them, maybe boiled with weeds, or served mashed up on a slice of bread, but Bibi won't make up her mind. Snail Man isn't any help; he's scared because a split has appeared in the base of his chair, exposing his spine to the cruelties of the world. Selfish pig, Magda thinks. Revenge is eating the cod heads by herself. She boils them and eats them plain.

The emptiness around them starts filling itself in, like a sketch in the process of accumulating splodges of coloured ink. A car arrives out of Nowheresville, its horn honking, with two soldiers on board, waving rifles stuffed with flowers. One of the soldiers plucks a crumpled lily out of his rifle and throws it at her feet. It is followed by a bar of soap. Magda hasn't seen soap for a long time, and, at first, the sight of it (and the smell of it) confuses her. Eventually, she remembers the use of the thing, and lathers it up into bubbles in the nearest puddle.

"Bibi, look. I'm getting clean. Remember clean?"

Her sister doesn't reply. She doesn't even bother opening her eyes. Her silk headscarf has fallen away, revealing wisps of hair and ugly, crusted-over sores. Magda rinses her hands in the puddle and then dries them on her jacket. More cars begin to fill the street, most of them commandeered by soldiers. Those on foot barely glance at the twins. They scoot past, eyes averted, concentrating on the next rumour and what it might bring: a pork chop, a pile of tripe, even a handful of coarse flour in a brown paper bag.

A few days later, she comes home from one of her scavenging trips and finds Snail Man has vanished into thin air. Maybe he's been trundled off on a cart like a bag of refuse. This happens, but usually only to the dead and the not so dearly departed. He has left his chair behind. Magda is very tired, so she turns it the right way up and sits down, trying to avoid the split in the seat. She can't face making another journey, so the buried sardines lie untasted, and her rag of a sweater stays unworn. The third time she washes with the flower soap, a jeep pulls up alongside her, and a man in a double-breasted suit hops out.

"Has this body been claimed?"

He nudges Bibi with the toe of his polished brogue.

"Stop it! Can't you see she's sleeping."

He looks at her funny. Magda remembers the look, because it's the same one Uncle Erhard adopted when she told her stories (which he always called lies). A pause whilst the stranger adjusts his tie and calls over to the other people sitting in the jeep. Another man with a clipboard gets out the vehicle, along with a small woman, almost the same size as Magda, dressed in a print frock and a felt hat.

"Who is she?" The woman pulls a face as she looks down at Bibi. "Good God, somebody please cover the poor wretch up."

The man with the brogue shoes tosses his jacket over Bibi's face.

"You understand, don't you, young lady?"

Magda understands many things, of course she does. She knows, for example, how it all began; right from the get-go, she and her sister fought for air, for space, for love, and for freedom from the tyranny of each other's pea-in-the-pod sameness. And then one lost her voice and the other her shadow and suddenly, inexplicably war was something that raged outside them both. There is another journey to make now, and it is the first Magda has ever made alone. It is a journey into the future.

The future is a building with long corridors and many other children who are a little bit like her, but not enough for comfort, or friendship. She steals the marbles they play with and hides them behind the peeling wallpaper. The marbles rattle and roll, slipping out from their hiding places when icy draughts seep into the endless corridors. Each one is a different memory, and each rolls past Magda's desperate fingers, and out of her grasp.

Emma Staughton

Emma Staughton was born in Plymouth and graduated from Oxford Polytechnic in 1988 with a BA (Hons) in Architecture. After working in London and New Zealand, Emma moved to Cornwall in 1999 and rediscovered a childhood passion for writing. In between building projects, and with encouragement from her husband and book club, she completed a Masters in Creative Writing at Plymouth University in 2014, graduating with a first. Emma has written poetry, a novel and ten Cornish-based short stories. She lives on a farm near St. Austell with her husband and two dogs.

The Changeling

Carn Brea: 50°13'16"N 5°14'56"W

THE FIRST time I saw my mother panic was the day my baby sister almost drowned. I remember the smell of pine needles and chlorine. And the way my mother ran and jumped without a word, her pleated skirt an orange halo in the blue until it shrivelled with her to the bottom of the pool. My father glanced up from his newspaper with a look of mild surprise. Everything was quiet and uncertain until Mum surfaced holding Lara high like footballers do with trophies on the telly.

Is she OK? Dad hadn't budged. He was a large man who needed a good reason to shift from a comfortable position.

Mum's silence was white-faced. Normally she went red when she was upset, but that day she was white as she waded in slow motion to the swimming pool steps. Her bra showed through her wet blouse and her skirt stuck to her legs like orange cling film.

The first word my mother spoke was my sister's name.

Lara! For God's sake. Breathe!

Mum laid the limp body down on the sun-warmed concrete paving. Her voice was different – it was high-pitched and shaky, and the sound of it made my throat feel funny.

Dad raised himself from the plastic lounger and walked towards them. Mum pushed him away with a violent shove against his legs. She turned

Lara on her side and slapped her back, then flipped her over and kissed her on the mouth for a long time. It was weird. And all the time, Dad stood watching. Until Lara coughed and coughed and water spewed across my father's bare feet.

I'll get a towel, he said, and wandered off. That's when Mum lost it.

Don't you dare! She screamed. Don't you dare do that. Your daughter almost drowned and you did nothing. Nothing. I left you in charge for five minutes. Five minutes! Don't you dare walk away.

Jenny, stop it. My father's voice was low and stern. You're making a spectacle of yourself.

Friends from Redruth School were there with their parents. I don't remember names or faces. What I remember is my mother's fear, unmasked and raw on a summer's afternoon, and the shame of it.

About the same time the following year, I was lying in the garden making faces out of clouds as they streamed across the moor. It was a Saturday afternoon in June. A train passed on the main line, half a mile away, and a cockerel crowed from the village. My brothers were playing in their den at the bottom of the garden beneath the elderflower bushes. Mum had picked all the elderflowers in the midday sun and boiled them with lemon and sugar to make Elderflower Champagne, my favourite drink. Dad was inside watching football on the telly. The sitting room doors opened onto the garden patio and I could hear the occasional roar from the TV crowd and loud curse from my father when the wrong team scored.

The front door banged shut on the far side of the house. Mum was home from the hairdresser. She would go upstairs to check on Lara before saying hello to us. Ever since the incident at the pool, she fussed more and more over my younger sister. Lara had her own bedroom looking up at the castle on the moor. My brothers and I shared a dormitory with a Velux-framed view of the sky.

She's a child who needs her sleep, Mum would tell people. Lara did sleep a lot, it was true. When her eyes were open, they were blue as the skies above Carn Brea. She had tight red curls, a freckled face and a silent rosebud mouth. She was almost three years old and we were still waiting for her to speak.

I resumed cloud watching – there was a man with a beard growing in the sky, and a woman, except she was changing into a horse, or was it a dog?

Is Lara out there with you? Mum and her new hairdo were leaning out of Lara's bedroom window and there was an edge of concern to her voice.

No, I answered. I thought she was asleep upstairs.

Mum's head disappeared. Everything went quiet. It was a warm day and only the velvet bees had the energy to buzz. That was until my parents starting screaming at each other.

I leave you in charge for one hour and this is what happens! Where is she, Bobby? Where is Lara? You must have heard something. Seen something.

Calm down, said Dad. Why is everything such a bloody drama with you, Jen? And keep your voice down, or the neighbours will hear.

I want the bloody neighbours to hear, said Mum. I've searched the entire house and Lara's gone. I want the whole world to hear. 'Phone the police, Bobby. Call them right now. My mother's voice was shrill.

The patio doors closed with a loud thud and the noise of their voices faded. I crept into the house through the back door and heard my mother on the telephone.

Jenny Trayer. My name is Jenny Trayer and my three-year-old daughter is missing.

Mum's voice was calm, but I could tell she was making an effort because there was a tremor to it. Upstairs, my father was opening and closing doors and calling Lara's name. He leaned over the banisters.

Why are you calling the police, for god's sake? We haven't even checked the garden or asked the neighbours, yet, Jen.

I hovered in the hallway and watched my mother's face. She looked up at my Dad. I couldn't tell if she was talking to the police or my father, but she was whimpering like a puppy with the telephone receiver clutched to her cheek.

I know something's happened to her. I have this dreadful feeling. I'm her mother. I just know.

The police found Lara asleep in next-door's dog basket. Nobody knew how she got there because she was too small to reach the latches on the front door or garden gate. George and Marjory Peters, the neighbours, had a pug called Pug. And that's where she was – curled up with Pug under a crab apple tree in next-door's garden.

That night, Lara wouldn't go to sleep. She climbed the stairs to our attic dormitory and jumped on the beds, giggling. When we tried to take her back to her bedroom, she screamed. It took two more nights like that to make Mum cross. Mum took her to bed and she came right back down the stairs. Mum carried her back up. She slid down on her behind. Mum smacked her legs. Lara cried and ran to Dad. Then Mum cried, too, and turned away to blow her nose.

I just wish she could talk, said my mother.

Talk!

We all looked up. I was trying to do my geography homework at the kitchen table. The boys were building a Lego spaceship and Dad had been reading the papers, before Lara climbed on his lap.

Lara Talk!

There was no stopping her after that. Mum said she was like a sponge sopping up words. My three-year-old sister wanted to know the name of everything that lived and breathed, and everything that didn't.

I had learned a new word at school. Bosoms. I kept saying it in my head and if nobody was listening, out loud. Bosoms. Bosoms. It made me feel funny when I said it – like I wanted to wee, except I didn't. Bosom was the grown-up word for boobies, and I knew what they were because my Uncle Colin told me.

Let's see your boobies, Karen, and check if they're growing, he'd say. I would lift up my T-shirt so that we could inspect them together in the bathroom mirror. I liked my Uncle Colin. He was handsome and let us stay up late and take puffs on his cigarettes when he came to babysit. He read us Tales of the Unexpected, which was scary but fun, even though the stories gave us nightmares. He made us keep secrets, and even that was fun. Our check-the-boobies sessions were one of his little secrets.

I taught Lara how to say 'bosoms' and we looked in the bathroom mirror to see how hers were growing. Mum found us in there one day touching each other's nipples.

Karen. What are you doing? She sounded cross. I told her Uncle Colin had said it was OK. She looked very serious, but spoke in a gentle voice.

Karen, love, I'm going to put Lara to bed and then I need to have a little talk with you.

Later, she sat me down at the kitchen table and asked weird things that made me stare, hot-faced, into the fruit bowl. We never saw Uncle Colin again after that. I felt guilty. He had asked me to keep a secret and I had betrayed him.

Waking became my favourite moment, because Lara was asleep. I crept downstairs, unlocked the patio doors and walked across the silver lawn. The grass was dew-damp between my toes until I reached the path, then gravel made me hop from foot to foot. There was a meadow at the bottom of our garden where donkeys grazed. They had pale grey coats and Jesus crosses on their backs. I stroked their soft noses and scratched them behind their ears. They drank from a trough against our fence. A family of crows drank from it, too. Most mornings, I found islands of bird poo floating across the surface like little jellyfish. I kept a plastic jug in the hedge and enjoyed bailing the trough to make it gurgle and fill with sparkling water. But that morning I had no time for cleaning because I had come to speak to the Little People about my sister.

It had been two weeks since the family had slept. Lara no longer needed sleep. She needed games, songs, stories, TV, ice-cream, toast with marmite, toast with strawberry jam, peanut butter. The 'No' word made her wild and she would scream, red-faced, and hit anything that moved, usually my brothers and me. Lara just wasn't Lara any more.

Beyond the donkey meadow, the earth grew into a large mountain with a castle and a big stone cross. Mrs Moore said Little People lived on the mountain. She was my teacher and I believed her. There were piskies in the trees and spriggans behind the boulders. Spriggans did bad things like kidnap children's brains when they were sleeping. I decided Lara's brain had been kidnapped the day she disappeared and turned up in Pug's basket, next door. If I sat quietly, I might see a spriggan and beg him to put old Lara back inside her head.

I said hello to the donkeys and sat in the grass, waiting. It was tempting to cloud watch, but I had to concentrate. Mrs Moore said Little People were difficult to spot, but they could always see us. Soon, Lara would be awake, asking questions and patrolling the garden looking for me. I told my troubles to the donkeys and asked them to tell the Little People.

I did this three mornings in a row, and then I waited for a miracle.

Mum thought Uncle Colin had something to do with Lara's behaviour. I overheard her talking to Dad one night.

He's been babysitting the girls for two years, for god's sake, she said. If he's touched Karen, then he's sure as hell touched Lara. The poor child was too young to speak. Too young to tell us what was happening.

She can speak now all right, said my father.

Yes. But, the damage is done, isn't it? She's traumatised, said my mother. She's blanked the whole thing out.

You don't know that, said Dad. Colin might be an idiot, teasing Karen about her breasts, but he's no paedophile.

How do you know? My mother's voice had risen. It frightened me when she got upset – the world felt scary and I had a sick feeling in my tummy.

The next day, I asked Mrs Moore what a paedophile was. It was the last day of term and we had just packed up our desks and were filing out of the classroom. Everyone was laughing and chatting, except me.

Is there anything wrong, Karen? Mrs Moore asked. You've not been yourself recently.

Mrs Moore, I said. What does paedophile mean?

Mrs Moore looked flustered.

Oh, that's a long word for a little girl, she said. Where did you learn such a word?

I told her about Mum and Dad and Lara and Uncle Colin. Mrs Moore's lips shrank into a tight, wrinkled hole that reminded me of Pug's bottom below his curly tail.

Mum and Dad spoke in hushed voices after that. A woman called to talk to us. She was dressed in a suit like a man, but with a woman's hairdo, sort of puffy and big. Mum looked nervous and kept offering the woman cups of tea and chocolate biscuits. The woman asked more questions about Uncle Colin while Lara ate all the biscuits and smeared chocolate over the sofa arm.

There, there. Never mind, said Mum, which was weird because normally she would have been really cross.

I told the woman in a man's suit that it had all been a big mistake and Uncle Colin was really nice and kind. It was the spriggans who had stolen my sister's brain and made everything horrible.

A week later, we all went to the doctor's. Except he wasn't a proper doctor and Mum said there was nothing wrong with us. We visited his office in Truro – it was like a big sitting room with sofas and dolls for us to play with. It was fun, until the man asked more questions about Uncle Colin. His breath smelled like hard-boiled eggs and I pretend to be dumb. Mum ended up crying a lot and talking to him more than we did. Lara broke the head off a Cindy doll and the man wrote things down in his Exercise Book. Then we left.

That summer, we went to St Euny church every Sunday. Dad came too. The first time we visited, Dad showed me the big granite seat under the church porch.

It's called a coffin rest, he said. It's much longer than most coffin rests. Do you know why that is?

It's for a giant coffin, I said.

Dad laughed.

You're a clever little thing. He tousled my hair and I felt proud.

No, he said. It's for when they bury lots of people, like after a mining disaster.

Bobby! Don't tell the children things like that, said my mother.

You can't shelter them forever, Jen. It's history. Mining is part of their heritage. My grandfather was a miner, and his father before him.

While they were bickering, I walked the length of the coffin stone and decided I was right. It was definitely made for giants when they died.

Inside, it was a happy church. Light streamed through big, arched windows. You could see trees and clouds through the clear glass – some churches had coloured glass that blocked out the sky and made me feel sad. The singing was my favourite part. The sound of the organ made my chest feel fluttery, as though a bird was trapped inside. But the prayers were old-fashioned and boring. While everyone was kneeling on red cushions, mumbling, I prayed to Jesus and the Holy Dove to make the spriggans bring Lara's brain back.

After the service, Mum and Dad drank tea and coffee with everyone at the back of the church. Lara and the boys played hide and seek amongst the pews and I escaped outside. The metal side gate squeaked open and clanked shut. The graveyard was my secret garden and I was hidden in a forest of fern, pink campion and cow parsley. As I pushed through a tumble of wild flowers, I stroked mossy gravestones and tried to read the frilly words. Everything looked ancient and undisturbed. This was the Little People's garden, I felt certain of it, and said another prayer.

Marjory Peters suggested Mum get a pet for Lara. We visited the big pet shop in Camborne. It smelled of sawdust and poo, and there were jungle noises coming out of the ceiling. We watched gerbils behind glass screens tunnelling through sand, and floppy-eared rabbits that didn't do much. There were white mice with pink noses crawling along plastic corridors, and podgy hamsters galloping on the spot in yellow wheels. Lara wanted a red and green parrot called Charlie, who shrieked incessantly.

We departed with a guinea pig each and a large hutch. Dad spent the weekend making a guinea pig run out of wood and chicken wire, and by Sunday lunchtime our new pets were skipping around the lawn, chattering with pleasure.

A week later, I woke late and rushed down the garden path to clean the donkeys' water trough and pick grass for the guinea pigs. As I started bailing, Lara appeared.

What's that? She pointed at a dead beetle floating in the water.

It's a beetle that drowned, I said.

Why did it drown?

It couldn't breathe in the water, I suppose.

But, it's swimming, she said.

No, it's dead, I said. It only looks like it's moving as I bail.

I captured the creature in a jug of cloudy water and poured it onto the grass.

There, you see. It's dead.

What's drowned mean? Lara prodded the beetle.

I sighed and tried to explain, but gave up and walked off to feed the guinea pigs and clean out their cage. They heard me coming and chattered and squeaked in greeting from the darkness of their hutch. I lifted each guinea pig in turn for a cuddle before placing it in the garden run. I cleaned out the hutch and made a fresh hay nest in their sleeping compartment. Then I went inside to get dressed before breakfast.

Where's Lara? said Mum. She was laying out plates of poached eggs on toast around the kitchen table. Dad had already left for work.

I was about to tell her, when Lara appeared at the door soaking wet.

Look at you, child, said Mum. Come on. Let's get some dry clothes on you.

Pigs swimming! Lara pointed towards the end of the garden.

What did you say? Mum and I spoke in unison, but my mother moved faster than me. By the time I had looked in the empty guinea pig run and checked the hutch, Mum was barring my way at the bottom of the path, white-faced.

Karen, she said. Go back inside the house. Back inside, now!

Lara had followed us down the path.

Pigs swimming, she said, pointing towards the water trough. And then she laughed. My mother grabbed her by the arm and Lara squealed. I pretended to walk away, then doubled back and peered over the hedge. I watched my mother drag Lara towards the water trough. On the ground lay four sodden bodies. They looked too small to be guinea pigs, and for a moment I thought Mum had made a mistake and they were rats. Without a word, my mother pushed Lara into the water trough. Pushed her in and pushed her under.

Things were better after that. Mum said it was my scream that stopped her. I told her it wasn't me who screamed, but she didn't believe me. I told her it was the spriggans screaming from the moors to save their child from drowning. But that just annoyed her.

Every morning, I walk across the silver lawn and down the gravel path to tell the donkeys to tell the Little People how happy we are to have gentle, sleepy Lara back. Silent Lara.

End Notes/Glossary for 'The Changeling'

- 'The Changeling' is based on William Bottrell's 'The Changeling of Brea Vean' from his 1870 collection of anecdotal stories: 'One day in harvest time a woman called Jenny Trayer, who lived at the foot of Carn Brea, fed her baby and rocked it to sleep, and then went out to help with the reaping. When she returned, the cradle was overturned and the baby was missing. Then, searching around the cottage she found the child asleep in a corner. But the baby never seemed right to her after that – it was always unhappy and bad tempered...' [Bottrell, Vol. 2, 201]

- Brea: means 'Hill' in Cornish. Brea Vean, means 'Little Hill'. Carn means 'Rock Pile'. [Holmes, 17-19]

- Carn Brea: 'The summit of Carn Brea is one of the great viewpoints of Cornwall with the sea visible on both N and S horizons on a good day. The eastern two of three tors constitutes the most fully excavated early Neolithic tor enclosure in SW England'. [Pevsner, 147]

- Carn Brea Castle: a Gothic folly rising from the boulder-strewn summit of Carn Brea, built by the Basset family to resemble a Norman keep, C18/C19. [Pevsner, 147]

- Little people: or 'small people' – faeries, piskies, knockers, spriggans – said to be the ghosts of pagan ancestors from a prehistoric Cornish race, now spirit guardians of the landscape. [Gary, 43-48]

- Carn Brea Monument: a tapering octagonal Celtic cross on the summit of Carn Brea. This monument to Francis Basset of Tehidy (Lord de Dunstanville) was built in 1836. 'Its scale a suitably imposing testimony to the power and wealth of one of the greatest of all the Cornish mining dynasties.' [Pevsner, 147]

- St. Euny Church: located in Churchtown, below Carn Brea. Known as 'The Mining Church' due to its proximity to the Great Flat Lode, Cornwall's greatest mining area. Pevsner describes it: '...set within a lovely embowered churchyard. The tall, elegant late C15 W tower of granite ashlar has buttresses set back from the angles and angel corbels to the corners of the embattled parapet, from which crocketed pinnacles crown slender turrets.' [Pevsner, 468]

- Coffin Rest: 'The unusually long coffin stone in the lych gate [of St. Euny's] is said to be for funerals where several coffins would be brought in together. In August, 1883, an accident at Wheal Agar in Pool killed twelve men at once... as you walk here, remember those who died in an industry that brought great wealth and opportunity, but which caused great wounds still felt today.' [From an inscription outside St. Euny Church.]

Emma Timpany

Emma Timpany was born and grew up in Dunedin, New Zealand. She loves reading short stories as well as writing them. Her stories are published in the collections *The Lost of Syros* (Cultured Llama Press) and *Over the Dam* (Red Squirrel Press). Her novel, *Travelling in the Dark*, is forthcoming from Rosa Mira Books. *Flowers* was inspired by her experience of working as a flower grower in Cornwall. She's currently working on a full-length work of fiction which further explores her own, and her family's, experiences as florists and flower growers. https://emmatImpany.wordpress.com

Flowers

This is the place: four fields in the shape of a rough parallelogram. On her left, one area of the closest field is enclosed behind wire mesh. A path runs through long, wet grass towards a gate in the fence. Ahead of her is an open-fronted barn with a caravan parked inside it, a chimney rising from its roof.

She cannot see anyone. She is about to leave when, looking again, she notices a figure kneeling inside the fencing.

She walks over but he does not seem to know she is there. He wears a suit, some kind of woollen weave, not tweed.

Hello.

Hello.

He is young, younger than her. He stands and wipes his hands on his clothes. His hair is flat and yellowish. Despite his smile, his face is the wrong kind of white. He has been ill. Is still ill, perhaps.

Rachel said you wanted someone to grow flowers.

Yes. He shakes his head as if confused. I only just woke up. I still have to sleep a lot. But I remember now.

She doesn't know what to say. She doesn't know what she was expecting but it was not this.

Are you cold? he says. It's cold today.

And bleak, she does not say, this place is bleak.

Let's have some tea.

The barn smells of dirt and straw, the caravan of damp. His bed is a heap of sleeping bags and blankets; the cups are stained with a thick layer of tannin. Roll-up butts huddle, crushed together in a jar lid.

Sit down. Here. He moves a pile of books from a seat. Rachel said you were a florist.

Well, yes. Sort of. I never meant to be. It wasn't what I wanted.

He lights the camp stove, rolls a cigarette.

My family were. Florists, I mean. My grandfather lost his job in the Great Depression. Five kids and nothing to eat. So my grandmother started growing flowers. She doesn't know why she is telling him this. She doesn't tell anyone this. She shakes her head.

I don't have any biscuits.

It doesn't matter.

I only have goat's milk. Is that ok?

Yes. She has never drunk goat's milk. That's ok.

It is raining. In her mind the earth has a red tint but now she sees that, under the rain, the soil is deep brown, black, almost. He has laid out some beds within the wire mesh, six rectangles of soil. The fence is to keep out the rabbits which will otherwise eat everything.

Look. He points to a line of feathery green leaves. I planted them in December and they're up already.

Are they a type that grows in winter?

No. I was late putting them in because I was in hospital. All this should have been done earlier, in the autumn. This soil must be good soil.

It looks like good soil but she will not know until she starts to work it. The rain is heavy now, too heavy for her to begin.

In the shelter of the barn, he shows her rows of tools. Most are old but some are new, their dull silver light an oddity amongst the rest, the well-used and the worn.

The next time, there is no sign of him, though she scans the field for a crouched figure in a suit. Inside the barn, still air that could mistakenly be called warm but is only the cessation of wind. Through the window, she sees him curled up on his side, blankets heaped around him, holes in the bottom of his socks.

She climbs over the rabbit fence and puts a bin bag, filled with bags of bulbs and packets of seeds, down by the side of the bed of freshly dug earth he indicated, last time, that she could plant. Returns to the barn for tools along the path of beaten grass. Begins to mark out a row.

The rows of vegetables in the neighbouring beds are all perfectly straight. By contrast, the trench she has made wavers. She goes back to her row and tries to even it up, mentally making a list of the things she will need – bamboo poles, string.

The soil smells slightly of iron, of leaves. Small stones appear occasionally but it has a lightness to it. She opens a packet of bulbs – tulips – and looks at them in the dim light. It is three months past the optimum time to plant them. She bought them cheaply from a local discount store but they look in good condition, a bright brown, shiny sheath on the outside of the pure white bulb. Plant at twice the depth of bulb. She lays them out fifteen centimetres apart then covers them.

The beds are larger than she thought. She adds sawdust to the list in her head. The last seeds she plants are poppies. Light, tiny, they are indistinguishable from the soil as soon as she sows them.

You've been busy. He is wearing an old oilskin over his suit.

Yes.

What have you been planting?

Bulbs, she says. Seeds. She fumbles for the packets and hands them to him. Her jeans are soaked from where she has been kneeling.

These are nice. He holds the empty poppy packet.

They were free. I wouldn't have bought them. Because the flowers only last a day or so. Still, I can use the seed heads.

That's a shame. About the flowers.

It's often the way. The most beautiful don't last.

He is looking at her rows.

I should have made them straight. Next time I'll bring some string.

I've got some. Poles and string. Didn't you see them in the barn?

No.

Before he got ill, he tells her, he was a set designer. Now he works on the field. The quiet here, the growing things. It is his way of making himself better.

Look, peregrine.

She does not want to look but, raising her head, she follows his finger to where the bird flies through veils of rain.

We should go in. Shelter from this. Do you want tea?

No, thanks. I'm soaked. She is cold now, having been still for so long. The thought of sitting in the caravan is not a pleasant one. I'll be back next week.

She knocks mud off the spade and fork and carries them back to the barn. He opens the caravan door; warmth from the camp stove drifts out. Condensation fogs the windows. He is smiling at her, and she wonders what he is going to say.

Could you bring some milk when you come next time? I can't have dairy. Goat's milk. Or soya.

Sure, she says.

Back at the car she takes off her gumboots, her soaking coat, and loads them in the boot. Strips off her jeans and wraps her lower half in a blanket. Drives home that way.

From the highest point, where she now stands, and the high point opposite her, the land creases down, as if it has been folded on the diagonal, into the corner farthest from her. Because he is working near the bottom of the crease, it is hard to make out what he is doing.

She has forgotten the milk.

It has already started to bother her that it is his soil, his earth, his rules. That she is merely scratching, borrowing a few centimetres of surface. And yet she cannot imagine belonging to this place, it being hers. It is not what she would choose for herself. It is too high, too exposed. The jumbled boulders of the carn seem, at times, a reflection of her confusion. And then there is the cold, a deep earth-and-stone cold, the kind that gets in your bones. She wonders again what is wrong with him, what was wrong with him.

The quiet, though, also has a way of its own. In the way her life is away from this place, it feels like nourishment. Every action she initiates proceeds, un-thwarted, until it is complete. No-one else to consider except for the too-thin man she sees out of the corner of her eye.

She is planting *Liatris spicata*. The bulbs are dark, knobbly, a light hair of old, dried roots on their bases. Their hairiness reminds her of sea potatoes, found on the nearby beaches at low-tide. When she looks up she notices two parallel rows of bamboo canes, joined at their apex, stand in one of the beds. Supports for beans, perhaps, or peas. Everything he does out here, in the beds, is so neat. But it is not neat in the barn or in the caravan.

No rain today but it is cold. Smoky-yellow light crouches at the edges of the sky. A row of *Camassia leicthlinii*, a cultivar of quamash. The bulbs are white and smooth, small green shoots already sprouting from their apical points. It is far too late to be planting them. She tries to think of May, when these bulbs will produce long straight green stems, and then star-shaped flowers, blue and cream.

She hears the soft sound of his boots on the grass. As she turns, reluctant to stop her work, she briefly wonders what he thinks of her. Her neck aches, so she rubs it.

More bulbs.

Yes. Look at these. She lifts an *Eremurus stenophyllus* tuber from brown paper, holding towards him the flat disc with leggy roots, like the dried limbs of a once fleshy spider.

And they'll stay in the soil? Or will you lift them?

No. They'll stay. They form clumps. Bulbs like these, perennials, reproduce themselves asexually. Clone themselves, basically. So you get more flowers year on year.

This seems to surprise him. She has no idea what he knows or doesn't know about flowers.

The next time there are lots of people at the field. It takes her a while to find him. People talk to her, seem interested in what she is doing. They tell her things about the man who owns the field, assuming she knows more than she does; without her prompting his secrets spill out on the grass. They all seem excited by the fact that their friend has this surfeit of space. Many of them live on boats, in vans and caravans squeezed into corners of fields, fringes of towns and villages.

She sees him in the distance, reassesses his age down a notch and then down again. How aged he is by illness, by the experience of illness. It makes him more like her; it is the bridge that links her on one side and his friends on the other.

She has found out, quite recently, that her brother has been lying to her. For years, he has stolen from her, from the joint assets left to them by their parents. He calls what he did an act of love. It is not love. There is a chance that she will lose her house, lose everything she has worked for.

The friends start dragging dead wood into a circle. Someone sets light to it. Bottles appear and a keg of beer. She plants *Nectaroscordum siculum*, an onion-paper fine sheath over its bulbs, which will one day be a handful of purple and green striped bells dangling from a wiggly stem. By the time she finishes, darkness is come. She looks over to the circle of light. The flames give his face the colour it normally lacks; she catches a glimpse of how he must have looked and how he might, perhaps, look again one day.

In the weak sunlight, the green tips of the first bulbs she planted poke through the earth, cast tiny purple shadows on the soil and she sees what he has described to her but she has never really believed. There is a view of the sea. Distant; complex with lines of trees and land in the foreground and further back, a skewed triangle of mint green water, a violet horizon.

Tomorrow, February tips into March. In the soil she finds a lime green grub, curled and sleeping. More seeds have broken through the earth; tiny as watercress, they tremble as if exhausted by the division of their first leaf into two. In the hearts of the hyacinths, flower spikes push upwards.

She knocks on the caravan door. No reply. She opens it, pulls a pint of goat's milk from her pocket, leaving it on the floor where she hopes he will see it.

The goat's milk was fresh today 28/2. See you next week?

She is annoyed that she brought him milk and he isn't here. But she is also pleased. Words have stopped, are trapped inside her. She does not want to talk. She wants to plant flowers, row and rows of flowers, and wait and watch and tend them as they grow.

Thank you for the milk.

I didn't bring any today.

What are you planting?

Lavender. She has bought plug plants and potted them on, hardened them off in her courtyard garden; against the vastness of the field, they seem tiny. She plants them through a layer of weed matting, cutting crosses and slotting one plant into each gap.

How long will they last for?

They'll grow and get bigger for about ten years or so. And then they'll die off.

As the day ends, she hears the sound of cars, footsteps and voices echoing down the track, the clink of bottles. The friends build a fire with new, dry boughs. The friends distract him, keep him busy, talking. In the fading light, he shifts from old to young, young to old.

Her back aches. She tidies her things and looks at what she has achieved. There is little to see; the bulk of her labour lies beneath the darkening surface of the soil.

The sky is a serious blue, which means darkness is not far away. Through the still air she hears the sharp crackle of flames and smells dry wood burning.

Today she plants the last of the bulbs, some alliums, the *Triteleia laxa*, and the sweet pea seeds, pre-scored. The poppies and the cornflowers are through. The love-lies-bleeding. The soil is warming. The irises have produced grey, strap-fine leaves. A violet beetle scuttles away under her hand. An idea, a question, a friend of a friend – all of these things have led her here. Now, the hyacinths are opening. As she cuts through their thick, sappy stems, washes the dirt off the leaves and lower flowers, the few open bells release a clean, sweet scent.

He has also been planning and planting. She has helped him to lift off the turf and peel it back, in preparation for a second row of beds.

The weeds have started to grow; the perennial buttercup, its net-like roots spread horizontally, is particularly hard to shift. She tracks the white roots of dandelions, zigzags of light in the dark soil, their wounds leaking a milky sap.

He digs for a while and then he stops and coughs. Whatever is wrong with him is taking its time to give up its hold.

He has gone to drink water, hand resting on the tap until the coughing eases. His clothes still hang on him like the clothes on a scarecrow. When was he last well? When did he last live in a house? She considers this coldness, rising from the earth, his enemy. She thinks he does not do enough to protect himself against it. How can he become better if he is not warm?

How will he get better if he drinks from filthy mugs?

He has seen her looking at him and now he beckons her. She climbs over the fence, her shoulders tense.

He points to a new ridge of earth by the side of the barn. From here she can see thin sticks are planted in it.

Willows, he says.

They'll grow big.

I know.

Why here?

Because this is where the house will go.

You're building a house?

One day.

To live in?

Isn't that why most people build houses?

I thought…But she doesn't know what she had thought.

He begins talking about dwelling rights, planning permission. The house will be built out of straw bales, with wool as insulation.

A house made of straw. Hasn't he read The Three Little Pigs?

She cuts the *Camassia leicthlinii 'Alba'*, secures five stems with a rubber band and drops them in a bucket. The alliums are ready, tall Gladiator and the squat lavender starburst of *Allium christophii*. Once they are all cut and bunched, she moves them into the shade. Dahlia tubers lie in the trench. She covers them, then plants sedum around the edges of the bed, a type with purple-black leaves and, come September, small, hard, ruby flowers.

She is beginning to realise that he did not think she would plant anything permanent. He expected that she would grow flowers from seed and harvest them, an annual crop. There has been this miscommunication, right from the beginning, probably the result of her reluctance to talk, his assumption that flowers were grown in the same way as vegetables.

She tells herself it does not matter. Everything she plants, with a couple of exceptions, can be dug up again and moved. Like people, flowers travel: transplanted with care, they usually manage to re-establish themselves, to put down new roots.

Twice in her life she has tried to run away from flowers, the first time from her family's floristry business, the second time when, out of necessity, she worked as a florist in London. Yet here she is, back among them. They follow her, it seems. Or she, unwittingly, unwillingly, follows them. They present themselves to her as opportunities, the only options.

She knows their common and Latin names; some have been her companions since earliest childhood, their names learnt alongside her own; they have always been amongst the most important inhabitants of her world. The flowers she grows, that line up wonkily behind her back like a beautiful army, are not as delicate as they look. They are survivors.

She is ready to go. She walks over to where he is working, beside the willow bank.

Goodbye, she says.

I'm going to get a digger in, to grade the earth flat for the house, he says. I'll get them to scoop out a pond while they're here.

I brought you some milk, she says.

Come and see the pond, he says.

A shallow basin has been scraped out below the flower beds, the excess soil tipped at the southerly edge, building it up into a bank; the effect is pleasing, as if the far lip of the pond were somehow floating above the lower parts of the field.

In her childhood garden, there was a stream, dividing the formal beds around the house from the secret spaces of a stand of native bush. A simple bridge, arch-backed, connected the two worlds; she remembers what it was to paddle in that stream, the little beach of pale gold gravel it left before it exited the property, edged by a rustling screen of bamboo.

So water, yes.

Nothing exists without water.

So many things are flowering: *Liatris spicata, Eryngium planum*, nigella, cornflowers, sweet peas. She comes early to cut the flowers, weeds a little, covers the soil in mulch to stop it losing moisture to the sun, leaves by eleven or twelve.

When she hears the caravan door open she looks up, expecting to see him, but a woman emerges and walks towards the standpipe to fill the kettle.

Hello.

Who are you? the woman says.

I'm the one who grows the flowers.

He comes out of the caravan, rubbing his hair.

When you're finished, can you give Jo a lift back to town? he says. Are you finished?

Yes. Pretty much. Just tidying up.

We haven't had breakfast yet, Jo says. We haven't even had a cup of tea.

You can have breakfast when you get home.

Are you trying to get rid of me, Jo says, before I've had a cup of tea?

Of course not, he says. I'll make you some tea. Would you like tea?

No, thanks, she says. I'm going soon. But I brought some milk.

As she carries the flowers to the edge of the track, Jo sits on one of the benches by the fire circle and talks to her. The things Jo says are funny in a pithy kind of way. She's pretty, too.

He brings out two mugs of tea.

I'm off now.

Do you mind giving Jo a lift?

Not at all.

I think I'll spend the day here, Jo says, stretching and looking around. It's going to be a beautiful day.

Do what you like, he says. But you should know I've got work to do.

Don't mind me. Jo lies back on the boards, folding her hands over her ribs, shutting her eyes. I'll be just fine.

The pond water is pale bronze, the suspended particles of soil in it yet to settle. He is wading, thigh deep, forearms immersed, planting marginals below the surface. The scent of water is softly mineral, a note of freshness amongst the dry grass and the dust.

Flower buds form on the tiny lavender bushes; the leaves of the sedum are dark as wine. What is winter? Its memory lies in the earth, beneath the bark of the shrubs, the trees. It lies in leaves which tremble in the light. It lies in pollen, gold and grey, the bees collect and carry with them from flower to flower.

When she looks over to the pond again she sees him floating on his back, arms and legs splayed out, five-pointed as a fallen star.

On the final day, when she comes to dig up the last of the flowers, he is not there. He has gone to work in Greece for a while, Jo tells her. On a sustainable building project.

Jo stands in the doorway of the house made of straw. I've got a flat in a proper house again, she says. I'm moving on, too.

The wool they'd used as insulation had been full of moth larvae; they'd had a massive infestation, as well as trouble with mice.

What sort of trouble with mice?

They were falling out of the ceiling onto my face, Jo says, while I was asleep.

What can be done?

Jo shrugs. Perhaps the moths have got into the straw. Perhaps the house will have to be torn down, and they'll start again somehow. He's gone away to have time to think things through.

Time to think. She had had it, in the hours that she spent here on her knees, eyes on the ground, hands in the good earth.

The willows he grew from sticks reach above her head. The lavenders have filled out from tiny plugs to dense, thick pads. They will remain, along with some other plants that are difficult to shift. Though she tries to lift them carefully, she is bound to miss some bulbs. After she is gone, they will put up their heads each spring, aiming for the light.

Will he think of them as a nuisance?

Or a gift?

Her new garden is big enough to hold all these flowers.

She walks over to the pond. On its green-grey surface, water lilies float, white and cream and copper-red, stands of sedge and flag iris softening its edges, and she feels it, as she felt it when she was a child, flowers all around her: a sense of dissolution between here and now and whatever lies just out of reach.

Here.

Whatever has filtered down into the darkness has given life to flowers that open like a hand; in the centre of each a deepening of colour, which she can hear as if it were a sound.

Nothing exists without water.

She thinks of him and knows that he is well.

Alison Wray

Alison Wray grew up in London. She gained a BA and doctorate in Linguistics at the University of York, and now works at Cardiff University as a Professor of Language and Communication. As a researcher she has published contributions to understanding how language is learned and how communication is disrupted in dementia. Although she has reached the long list in three previous short story competitions, *Natural Order* is her first publication in creative writing. Alison is also an accomplished classical singer, performing art song, oratorio, opera and chamber music around the UK and, occasionally, more exotic places, including China and Kenya.

Natural Order

The swallows will not fly south this year. When the afternoons darken and the grass slows its race towards the hedge tops, still the air will ring with their chatter, as it does today. They will swoop and chase, as they do now, exuberant, believing in a never-ending summer. They will not feast on extra grubs to see them through to Africa, but only pick the tastiest morsels, trusting us to lay out rinds and nuts if snow should blow its way to us come Christmas.

The apples will not fall and will not rot along the lawn like last year, but stay upon the trees. At advent, should we think to string out lights, we'll need no pine, nor dangled baubles on it. Their sweet aroma in the dampening air will catch our breath with cider tones, as in the barn where once we loved.

The nervous mice will not assemble in the roof, not stretch and reach to pick at dozy flies, but clench their paws and pock the swooping owls aside, then scurry on across the frosted straw.

Low suns will not sustain their shameful grey beyond the trees, when daytime feels still young – but re-emerge for one last time, stark red against an unimagined blue, then fall without a fuss when we must sleep. And morning will be bright with watery rays across the fresh and vital air, remarkable and constant.

The postman will not climb the drive with cards and letters wrung from tearful hearts; no flowers left for us to find outside when we get home. None will need to phone, to say the things we never say. Across the street the timid neighbours will not duck away, to spare the painful pleasantries.

We will not change the subject, sidestep plans, or bravely talk of things that will not be. For they will, they will be, after all. You will not bravely comment I look well, nor grieve because my gleaming hair is gone. We will not need to look for hats.

At night, I shall not hate myself for burdening you with this. I shall not tell you not to mind, nor coax you to a life you do not want to see. We shall not have to second guess, avoid the cracks lest there are bears. For nothing that could end will end; all manner of things that can be well shall be, and so shall I.

The barn owl will not quarter on our land, nor foxes glint their evening eye around the coop. The clouds may glower but no rain will fall. The heron by the lake will watch in vain. The slinking giant circling us will lay his club upon the ground and leave.

We will unravel life and time, and weave another way. And I will stay. Here, in this perfect present, where the swallows swoop, and apples, set and swelling, gently take the breeze and curl it round the garden. I will stay, and you will stay, and all of this will stay.

And so, with this, the springtime, love, will bring a different newness. A cool, foreign time where lambs hobble, where bluebells sink useless roots into the road. Where buzzards circle and frown, where hares mistake their stomping grounds and run errant. Where streams, reversed, leap to clear the ragged stones and goad the weeds with clods of sludge. Where trout in the lake confuse in circles, while tadpoles plead, dry, for pools. Everything will stilt and clatter out along the painful year.

The sun will rise perplexed, range around looking for morning and tumble back to leave the world unwarmed. The moon will turn its face away, then catapult to Venus for a better home.

Down in the woods will rise cacophonous the anxious yelling birds, in query and despair.

And you and I will check our step and tilt our heads to hear.

And we will whisper, 'we were wrong. Bring back the order, let us now concede'. For what can ever be the same, when good things stay beyond their time? And crowd the space that calls the swallows back and draws the apple blossom's breath?

Jeremy Charles Yang

Jeremy Charles Yang is a young Chinese-British writer from Hong Kong, currently based in London. Having completed an undergraduate degree in Psychology at University College London, as well as publishing his first story, shortlisted in the UCL Publisher's Prize, Jeremy resolved to pursue a career in writing, in addition to his dreams of rock stardom and becoming a pirate. He is currently working on a series of short stories and two novels, both of which are taking a very long time. Piracy is beginning to look very appealing.

The Zoo

They say the chances of being attacked by a shark are about one in 3.8 million. I like sharks because they're cool. I don't like sharks because they're always waiting. Once you enter the ocean, you enter the food chain, and I get the feeling they're fully aware of that. They say that if you're about to be attacked by a shark, you should punch it in the nose. Or the eye. The eye is better, because sharks have a thing called a *nictitating membrane* which protects their eyes from thrashing fish, and if you punch it, the shark will get hurt and go away. If you punch the nose, it might only daze it, giving you a short moment to do something else. Have you tried punching in water? I have, at the swimming pool with Dad. Trust me, it's hard. In any case, that's what you're supposed to do when you're about to be attacked by a shark.

That's why, when Billy Michele came at me in the playground because I said he had conduct disorder, I threw my fist into his stupid ugly face.

Billy is just like a shark. He's big, fast, and his face is mostly made up of nose and teeth. Have you ever noticed how sharks always seem to be smiling? Billy smiles a lot too. They probably have a lot to smile about, getting to do whatever they like. Billy's ruled the playground ever since I've known him when I joined in fourth grade. Him and his band of sharks, going around, doing what they like, and always waiting – waiting for the right moment to strike. His skin is an ugly grey-white, and looks like it'd be hard and cold to touch. I was surprised when I felt how soft and warm he was when I landed that punch on his nose. I'd never punched anyone before. But that's what you do when you're fighting off a shark.

I tried to explain this to Mr Parker-Jones, but Mr Parker-Jones doesn't seem to understand why I thought it was okay to punch Billy in the face. Mr Parker-Jones keeps trying to tell me that Billy isn't a shark – he's a person. I asked Mr Parker-Jones if he'd ever seen a shark before, because Dad used to take me to see the sharks before he died, and Billy's definitely a shark. Mr Parker-Jones doesn't understand.

The truth is, Mr Parker-Jones doesn't understand, because Mr Parker-Jones is a dog. And dogs don't ever go swimming with sharks. If they did, they wouldn't be able to punch the shark in the eye or nose. Instant shark food. I figured a while back, the best way to handle a mutt like Mr Parker-Jones is to grab him by the balls, and squeeze them just hard enough to make him pay attention to you, show that you're in control. I tried doing it in class once to Mr Tsang. He didn't like it, and he sent me to the principal's office to see Mr Parker-Jones. He and my mom both said the same thing: "*you can't grab people by the balls*". But Mr Tsang seemed to forget all about my missing homework, so I call that a success.

But today, there's something off about Mr Parker-Jones. He keeps looking around, scratching his head like some nervous puppy, and even though he's speaking to me, he won't look me in the eye. He keeps looking at the phone and the door and the clock behind my head on the wall. It's like someone else has got his balls in a vice.

'Kevin,' he says to me, 'don't you understand what you've done?'

Mr Parker-Jones is sweating pretty hard behind his desk, and it's beginning to smell because it's now three in the afternoon and the sun's been coming through the window like a magnifying glass. I try once more to explain what I'd done, and tell him about Billy's conduct disorder. He gives me a funny look, but the moment I mention the sharks, he tells me to "shut up about the sharks, Kevin". Sometimes I wonder if he's sleeping with my mother.

Suddenly there's a woman screaming outside the office, and other people talking loudly. There's a man yelling too. Mr Parker-Jones' ears prick up at the sound, and he jumps up with a yelp from his desk, nearly knocking it, and everything on it, over with me. He rushes over to the door.

'WHAT THE HELL HAPPENED?' yells the man's voice.

'HOW THE FUCK COULD YOU LET THIS HAPPEN?' The woman is hysterical. I hear Mr Parker-Jones apologising and asking everyone to please calm down, before closing the door so that all I can hear is how angry everybody is.

I've never been alone in the principal's office, but I'm glad Mr Parker-Jones has closed the door. I can't hear myself think when people are being hysterical. I like to be able to hear myself think.

I like Mr Parker-Jones' office, because it's quiet. It's not that quiet today, because of the hysterical people outside, but usually it is very quiet, quieter than the classrooms or the hallways or the gym, or that humming noise at the swimming pool. Usually it's just the sound of the clock, ticking away, and Mr Parker-Jones talking to me about appropriate school behaviour, but I can usually drown this out if I'm thinking about something else.

Right now, I'm thinking about my hand. It's sore and pink and there are still little traces of blood around my knuckles. I thought it was Billy's before, but now I think it's mine. I think I caught some of his teeth. That's another reason why it's dangerous to punch a shark on the nose. I want to go to the nurse so that I can get a plaster, but they're still yelling out there and I'm not sure if I'm supposed to leave.

I stand up from Mr Parker-Jones' desk and walk to the window. The sun's shining bright on the steps of the school, and I can see all the other kids running out to meet their parents and go home. I sometimes wonder why they call it a "school of fish". A real school is nothing like that at all. I watch all the kids running down the steps in all-different directions – everyone is going everywhere. Or is it nowhere? These kids are nowhere near as smart as fish. I stop looking because they're making my head hurt. I start to count the colours of the cars in the car park so I don't have to listen to the yelling. Twelve grey, five blue, two red, six black. Mom's car is somewhere down there, I know it, camouflaged among all the others, one of the herd. But she always picks me up from school after work. The door clicks open and shut and I hear her voice.

'Kevin.'

Mom.

Her voice is soft today. That means something serious has happened.

I turn around and see my mom standing at the door of Mr Parker-Jones' office. She tilts her head slightly to the side and gives me that smile which always looks like it's being slowly, gently pulled across her face, like a smile that has to be there, but doesn't want to be. Like *me* being in Mr Parker-Jones' office. She takes a small step towards me.

'Oh Kevin, what did you do?'

What did I do? I'm not sure what to say, but she quickly comes over to the window and gets down on her knee, like she does, so she can hold my head on her shoulder. I don't know why I feel like crying. It's like I was supposed to this whole time. I cry a little, on to mom's shoulder – I always cry there.

'Shhh, shhh,' she pats my back like she always does, and I feel better.

The door suddenly bursts open, and two strangers storm into the office with Mr Parker-Jones.

'YOU LITTLE SHIT!' The woman is screaming. She's ginormous and her eyes are crazy wide as she stares at me. I feel like she's going to attack me, and I'm scared. Next to her, a man, tall, thin, with a nose-and-tooth-face like Billy's, holds the woman by the shoulder. He glares with one cold eye in my direction. He is not smiling. My mother stands up and puts her arms out in front of me, facing the two new people. I tighten my sore hand back into a fist, ready to defend myself the way I did with Billy. But I look at Mr Parker-Jones, his face pink and drenched with sweat, and I wonder to myself whether any of this is appropriate school behaviour.

He tries to calm everyone down, but the woman won't listen. She's crazy and takes a step towards me.

'You fucking little shit! How dare you! You little fucking psychopath!'

'Don't you DARE talk to my son that way!' yells my mother.

The big woman reminds me of a bear. She has her big bear paws raised halfway at her sides, her big bear arms swinging around as she's held back by the shark man.

'What the fuck did you do? What the fuck were you thinking, you crazy little-?'

She makes another step towards me. The best way to deal with bears is to play dead.

'Can you fucking hear me?! Are you fucking listening? What did you do to my son?!'

'Now, Mrs Michele, I can only imagine how you must feel right- '

'DON'T YOU TELL ME HOW I FEEL!'

My mother grabs me from the floor and lifts me into her arms. If the bear still comes at you, you stand tall and wave your arms to make yourself look as big as possible.

'What the fuck is he doing?'

'Jesus, what the fuck is wrong with your kid?'

'There's NOTHING wrong with Kevin!'

You don't look the bear in the eye, because it might think you're a threat.

'Jesus.'

But you stand your ground and keep waving.

'Mrs Davidson, I think it's best if you take Kevin outside for the moment.'

'Yes, thank you, Mr Parker-Jones.'

You're not supposed to run from a bear.

Obviously Mom doesn't know that.

The bear woman and shark man keep screaming and yelling as Mom carries me out into the hall. 'DON'T YOU DARE WALK AWAY FROM ME! YOU KNOW YOUR SON IS A FUCKING PSYCHO- '

The door shuts behind us and she sits us down on the benches outside Mr Parker-Jones' office. When she puts me down I look up and I see she's crying.

'What's wrong Mom?

Her face is wet and I notice that she cried on the shoulder of my shirt. It's warm and wet and feels weird.

'Oh Kevin,' she says again. 'What did you do?'

I'm finding it hard to hear myself think. I'm not sure why. It's quiet in the hall. Everyone's already left. I don't know what to say.

'Mom,' I say, 'do you know what happens to a shark when it stops moving?'

'Damn it, Kevin,' she sobs. 'Shut up about the damned sharks.'

I shut up about the sharks. A little because I'm thinking about Mom and Mr Parker-Jones again, but more because Mom never swears.

'Billy has conduct disorder,' I tell her. She doesn't look at me. She's staring somewhere in the direction of the lockers across the hall. I don't think she sees them though. There's a poster on the lockers in front of her telling people to vote for Leah Gould for class president. Her picture always makes me laugh because she's got buckteeth like a rabbit, and because presidents can't be eleven, but mom doesn't see it; she's not laughing.

'Billy's dead, Kevin.'

Billy was moving fast. I punched him in the face and stopped him from moving. When a shark stops moving, do you know what happens?

'I didn't mean to,' I tell her. She doesn't say a word, but she's stopped crying. She looks pink around the eyes, like Mr Parker-Jones' face and neck when he was sweating. I slip my arms around her waist and hug her tight.

'You know orang-utans are some of the best moms,' I tell her.

'Kevin- '

'They never put their babies down. Not until they're six or seven.'

'Please, Kevin- '

'They reach maturity when they turn fifteen, and if people mature between twenty and twenty-seven, that means- '

'Damn it, Kevin, I'm not an orang-utan! I'm your mother! Now let go of me, for fuck's sake!'

I let go. I look at her face and I don't think she knows what to say. Mom never swears.

I stand up. I want to go. I wish Dad was here. He knew about orang-utans. He showed me at the Zoo.

I have to go.

'Kevin! Wait!'

No.

'KEVIN! COME BACK!'

No. I'm running down the hall.

'KEVIN!'

Keep running.

I run through the hallway doors, quick as a mouse. She can't run as fast as me. No one catches a mouse when it's moving. They run around in the dark, when everyone's asleep, and they learn to know where and how to run. I'm the same. Like when I ask the teachers for toilet breaks. This is my burrow, and I know every twist and turn.

I can hear Mom chasing after me, but she doesn't know these tunnels, not like I do. I scurry down past the library and the science labs. Quick and quiet, I scuttle through the doors of the cafeteria, and crawl under the small table by the entrance where the lunch lady with the metal box sits. I'm like a turtle and the table is my shell.

'Kevin! Please, come back!' I know she's looking for me. But she won't get me. When a turtle goes inside its shell, nothing can make it come out until it wants to. I'm the same, and I'm not coming out.

Footsteps hurry towards the cafeteria. I stay still and quiet. I hear the footsteps pass the cafeteria doors and carry on down the hall. I stay still inside my shell. The shell keeps me safe. A turtle must wait until the time is right, before coming out of its shell (because they're also really slow on land).

I wait a few more minutes before slowly stretching my neck and head out so I can listen. All is quiet. I can hear myself think. When I'm ready, I crawl out from under the table, and step back into the hallway.

The hallway is silent too. Everyone has gone. Mom must be looking for me somewhere, but she won't find me. Not yet. She doesn't know I'm here. Mr Parker-Jones' won't find me either. Unless he's got a nose too.

I go left and walk down the empty hallway, past the empty classrooms, past the empty nurse's office. I don't think I need the plaster anymore. It still hurts a little though. I like school when it's quiet like this; usually, it is so noisy. That's why its fun to walk around during class. It's so peaceful. Maybe that's why the fish are so smart to stick together; in their schools, no one ever has to say a word. They can hear themselves think. Right now I'm thinking about fish and I need to pee. I walk towards the gymnasium changing rooms, and go inside the boys'.

The boys' changing room smells like Dad's socks after he'd been out on the boat. It's gross. It is empty here too, but I don't like it as much. The air seems hot and wet and it is a little harder to breathe. I open the next door.

The swimming pool. There's that humming again.

Hummmmmmmmmmmmmmmm.

Must be the thing that keeps the pool warm. I think that's what Dad said. He started playing 'shark' with me afterwards. It was fun.

'HELLO?'

It's echoey in here. No one's here. Empty. Empty everywhere.

Dad used to say not to go swimming without someone there because it's dangerous; you never know when an accident might happen. You could get hurt. I guess he was right. But sharks don't need help when they go swimming.

I take off my shoes and socks, because you're not supposed to swim with your shoes on. I take off my uniform too because I don't want to get them wet either, or Mom might get mad. Sharks don't wear shoes or uniforms. I slide into the pool. It's warm, thanks to the humming. I go in until the water is up to my nose. And then I stay still, until the water becomes still. I have to wait, and stay still. I'm a shark, and the water is my home.

I like sharks because I think they're cool.

Sharks are always waiting.

Judges' Profiles

Sara Davies (chair)   Sara is currently abridging and adapting fiction and non-fiction for radio readings and drama. She was a BBC Radio producer in Bristol from 1992 to 2013, working on documentaries, arts features, poetry programmes, dramas and readings for Radio 4 and Radio 3. She produced Radio 4 series including A Good Read, Book at Bedtime and Poetry Please, and directed around 60 Afternoon Dramas, Saturday dramas and 15' serials. She also commissioned and produced numerous short stories from many well-known and debut writers. Before working for BBC, Sara was a freelance reporter and presenter for radio (Woman's Hour, You and Yours) and television; she fronted a monthly arts programme for HTV for three years, and presented a number of social issue and arts documentaries for BBC and Channel 4. She also wrote for *The Guardian, The Observer* and various magazines.

Rowan Lawton   Rowan is a literary agent and the co-founder of Furniss Lawton – a literary agency that is part of the James Grant Group. She previously spent 10 years agenting at WME and PFD and represents writers of both fiction and non-fiction and her taste is wide-ranging. Rowan's clients include a number of debut novelists, including Bristol-based Emylia Hall, author of *The Book of Summers*, a Richard & Judy 2012 Book Club selection.

Sanjida O'Connell Sanjida is a writer and broadcaster. She's had four novels published, including *Sugar Island* and *The Naked Name of Love* (John Murray), and four non-fiction books; the latest two are: *Chimpanzee: The Making of the Film* (Disney) and *Sugar: The Grass that Changed the World* (Virgin Books). She writes on science and environmental issues for *The Guardian, The Independent* and *The Daily Telegraph*, and works as a wildlife presenter for the BBC. She has a PhD in Zoology and Psychology.

Nikesh Shukla Nikesh's debut novel, *Coconut Unlimited* was shortlisted for the Costa First Novel Award 2010 and longlisted for the Desmond Elliott Prize 2011. Nikesh, also, co-wrote a non-fiction essay about the riots with Kieran Yates called Generation Vexed: *What the Riots Don't Tell Us About Our Nation's Youth*, and a recent novella about food, called *The Time Machine*, donating all his proceeds to Roy Castle Lung Cancer Foundation. His latest novel is *Meatspace*, ("highly enjoyable." *The Guardian*) His short stories have been widely published and broadcast including in *Best British Short Stories 2013, Five Dials, The Sunday Times*, Book Slam and on BBC Radio 4. He has written for the *Guardian, Esquire* and BBC 2. He has, in the past, been writer in residence for BBC Asian Network and Royal Festival Hall. His Channel 4 Comedy Lab *Kabadasses* aired on E4 and Channel 4 in 2011. He hosts The Subaltern podcast. Guests have included Zadie Smith, Junot Diaz, George Saunders, Jennifer Egan and Evie Wyld.

Acknowledgments

Enormous thanks and appreciation to all those who have made this year's Bristol Short Story Prize possible through their commitment, hard work, kindness and generosity:

The judging panel – Sara Davies (chair), Rowan Lawton, Sanjida O'Connell and Nikesh Shukla. Our readers – Lucy Cowie, Katherine Hanks, Lu Hersey, Tania Hershman, Richard Jones, Mike Manson, Dawn Pomroy, Ali Reynolds. Chris Hill, Jonathan Ward, Imogen Clifton and the 3rd year Illustration students at University of the West of England. Arc Editorial Consultancy, Tangent Books, Bristol Central Library, Mel Harris at Waterstones, Peter Morgan and Mark Furneval at ScreenBeetle, Martin Booth and Joanna Papageorgiou at Bristol 24/7, Jane Guy and The Bristol Hotel, and Joe Burt, Annette Chown, Nicky Coates, Jessie Eames, Fran Ham, Sylvie Kruiniger, Marc Leverton, Kathy McDermott, Natasha Melia, Dave Oakley, and Thomas Rasche.

And a special thank you to all the writers who had the courage to enter this year's competition and gave us so many hours of wonderful reading.